"Carry me, Nick," Rachel appealed.

Nick took the child from Violet, Rachel's slender arms wrapping firmly around his neck, her soft breath whispering against his cheek.

Strange emotions welled up inside Nick's chest. He'd never held a child before, never felt the trusting way they clung, never smelled the scent of innocence that emanated from them. It was a strange feeling, one that sent pleasant warmth cascading through him.

He looked over at Violet, noting that the brilliant moonlight lovingly caressed her. She'd laughed a lot over the past couple of hours, and her laughter had been contagious. Her eyes had sparkled with her humor, and her lips entranced him as they'd curved upward in generous smiles. For a single moment, he'd wondered how they would taste. Sweet . . . Yes, they would definitely be sweet.

He quickly shoved that thought away.

Dear Reader,

Summer may be over, but autumn has its own special pleasures—the bright fall foliage and crisp, starry nights. It's the perfect time to curl up with a Silhouette Romance novel.

This month, we continue our FABULOUS FATHERS series with Nick Elliot, the handsome hero of Carla Cassidy's *Pixie Dust*. Under the influence of a little girl's charms and a mother's beauty, even a sworn bachelor can become enchanted by family life.

Love and miracles are alive and well in Duncan, Oklahoma! This little town with a lot of heart is the setting for Arlene James's brand new trilogy, THIS SIDE OF HEAVEN. The series starts off this month with *The Perfect Wedding*—a heartwarming lesson in the healing power of love.

In Elizabeth Krueger's *Dark Prince,* Celia Morawski accepts Jared Dalton's marriage proposal while tangled in the web of her own lies. But is it possible her prince has secrets darker than her own?

Be sure not to miss the fiery words and sizzling passion as rivals fall in love in Marie Ferrarella's *Her Man Friday.* Look for love and laughter in Gayle Kaye's *His Delicate Condition.* And new author Liz Ireland has lots of surprises in store for her heroine—and her readers—in *Man Trap.*

In the months to come, look for more books from some of your favorite authors, including Diana Palmer, Elizabeth August, Suzanne Carey and many more.

Until then, happy reading!

Anne Canadeo
Senior Editor
Silhouette Books

PIXIE DUST
Carla Cassidy

Silhouette
ROMANCE™
Published by Silhouette Books New York
America's Publisher of Contemporary Romance

To our Mimi, who brings magic to all of our lives

SILHOUETTE BOOKS
300 East 42nd St., New York, N.Y. 10017

PIXIE DUST

Copyright © 1993 by Carla Bracale

ISBN: 0-373-08958-9

First Silhouette Books printing September 1993

All the characters in this book have no existence outside the
imagination of the author and have no relation whatsoever to
anyone bearing the same name or names. They are not even
distantly inspired by any individual known or unknown to the
author, and all incidents are pure invention.

®: Trademark used under license and registered in the United States
Patent and Trademark Office and in other countries.

Printed in the U.S.A.

Books by Carla Cassidy

Silhouette Romance

Patchwork Family #818
Whatever Alex Wants... #856
Fire and Spice #884
Homespun Hearts #905
Golden Girl #924
Something New #942
Pixie Dust #958

Silhouette Desire

A Fleeting Moment #784

Silhouette Shadows

Swamp Secrets #4
Heart of the Beast #11

CARLA CASSIDY

Fourteen years ago, Carla Cassidy walked down the aisle to wed her own romantic hero. Much of her wedding day passed in a haze—she doesn't remember the kind of flowers she had, she doesn't remember the music. What she does remember is the look in his eyes as she approached. It was the look of love, and it's kept her happily married ever since.

Nick Elliot On Fatherhood...

To Rachel,

You fell asleep on my lap last night, your breath warming the side of my neck, your little hand resting in mine. I felt a sudden tightness in my chest, a fullness so great it almost scared me. Then I realized what I felt was love.

Who'd have thought a cynical divorce lawyer like me could so completely fall under the spell of one little fanciful girl and her beautiful mother?

I didn't believe in much of anything before you, Rachel, but with you sleeping in my arms, smiling in your world of fairy-tale dreams, I suddenly believe in magic. And when I look into your eyes, I see our future and know the magic is never-ending.

I guess I just wanted to tell you thanks for asking the pixies to make me your daddy. Every daddy needs a pixie princess, and I'm glad I've got you. I love you, kid.

Daddy

Chapter One

Nick Elliot awakened, becoming immediately disoriented when he realized he wasn't in his own bed in his Chicago apartment. Then he remembered—he was on vacation in Glenville, Ohio, staying in an old Victorian home owned by a widow named Violet. He'd flown in from Chicago late the night before, too late to meet his landlady. Janet, Nick's sister, who lived next door, had brought him in and gotten him settled while the widow woman slept.

He frowned, sensing somebody...something nearby. He cracked an eyelid, then jumped in surprise as he saw a little girl standing at the side of the bed, her bright blue eyes gazing at him solemnly.

She was a pretty little thing, with pale blond hair and delicate features. Obviously his landlady's granddaughter, he guessed, half sitting up to look at her. What the hell was she doing in here?

"Are you a monster?" she asked.

"Only when little girls wake me before I'm ready to get up," he grumbled.

"I don't like monsters," she said, looking at him with the piercing gaze only children possess. "I have pixie dust."

"Terrific," Nick replied sleepily, then yelped in surprise as she suddenly threw a handful of silver glitter over the top of his head.

At that moment a young woman flew into the room, her face blanching as she looked first at the little girl, then at Nick. "Rachel, what have you done?" She looked at Nick helplessly. "I'm so sorry...you must be Janet's brother, Nick. I'm Violet and this is my daughter Rachel...I'm really sorry uh...we...we have to go. We're going to be late." Tugging on Rachel's hand, she pulled the girl out of the room.

Nick sat there for a long moment, his mind reeling as he tried to assess what had just happened. When Janet had told him that she'd rented him a room from Violet Sanders, a widow who lived in the Victorian home next to her house, it had sounded like just what the doctor ordered. He could easily imagine this Violet. She'd probably have blue-tinted hair worn in a tidy little bun. She'd be plump from sampling all the cakes and pastries she loved to cook. The house would smell of warm gingerbread and sachet. After the past several years of his hurry-up, stressed-out life-style, it had all sounded magnificent.

He now stared at the doorway. Violet Sanders was nothing like he'd envisioned and he was disconcerted by the contrast between his imagination and reality. Her hair hadn't been blue-tinted, but rather, it was a pale corn silk that had waved softly to her shoulders. She'd been clad in a dark blue jogging suit that displayed the fact she didn't have a plump bone in her body.

He shook his head, completely disoriented by his strange wake-up call. He looked at his watch and groaned. It was just a few minutes after seven o'clock. He hadn't arrived here until almost two o'clock in the morning. He should go back to sleep, but he knew he wouldn't. His mind was already alert, brimming with questions. There was no way he'd be able to go back to sleep.

He got up and pulled on a pair of jeans, then headed downstairs, hoping he could locate the kitchen and get a cup of coffee. As he made his way down from his third-floor room, he noted that the house was very attractive. All the wood gleamed with polish, and the wallpaper all looked new.

He found the kitchen without any problem and eyed with distaste the congealed oatmeal in the pot on the stove. Janet hadn't told him what sort of arrangements had been made as far as meals, but he assumed he had kitchen privileges.

Back home in Chicago he rarely ate breakfast, never finding time for more than a fast cup of coffee usually drunk on the way to the courthouse.

He now poured himself a cup from the pot on the counter and sat down at the table. He decided the best way to officially start his vacation was to savor the enjoyment of lingering over a cup of hot brew.

He was still tired. He had a feeling that if he hadn't been awakened, he probably would have slept until noon. And what a strange wake-up call it had been. He shook his head, groaning as tiny bits of silver fell out of his hair and into his coffee.

Terrific. He got up and fixed himself more coffee, then carried it with him to the sink, gazing out the window that overlooked the backyard. It was a nice-size yard, although it had an aura of neglect. The grass needed mowing and there were several old flower beds containing the remnants of flowers long ago browned and dead.

He turned around as he heard the front door open, then close, and a second later Violet walked into the kitchen.

"Oh, you're up," she exclaimed.

"Hmm, I didn't really have a choice in the matter," he said pointedly.

Her face reddened slightly as she grabbed a cup and poured herself some of the coffee. "I'm really sorry about Rachel. She usually doesn't throw it on people... sometimes on Mr. Peabody, the hateful cat from next door, but I... She didn't mean anything by it—" She broke off, her blush deepening. "All I can say is that I'm sorry," she finally finished, her gaze going to his decorated hair.

"I suppose there's no real harm done," he replied grudgingly. "It will wash." He noticed how the sunlight streaming in the window played in her hair, turning its corn-silk color to shining strands of gold. It looked imminently touchable, as if it would be warm and soft and sweetly scented.

He shoved these thoughts out of his head, suddenly irritated that Violet wasn't old and gray-haired and matronly, aggravated that for just a moment he'd wondered how her hair would feel lying against his neck or tangled around his hands.

Maybe that glitter or whatever it was her daughter had thrown on him had addled his brain. What was he doing standing here in this strange kitchen entertaining fantasies about a woman he didn't even know, didn't want to know?

"I'm sorry I wasn't awake last night to welcome you properly," she said and he noticed that her eyes were the lavender shade of clouds at twilight. "When Janet called to tell me your plane was so late, she insisted I go on to bed and that she could get you settled in the room."

"I didn't need a welcome. All I needed was a bed." He knew he was being cranky, but he couldn't help it. Nothing was as he'd imagined. Even the house smelled differently than what he'd fantasized. Rather than a scent of gingerbread and lilacs, there was a biting odor of ammonia and the stronger scent of solvent. "What is that smell?"

She looked at him in surprise. "What smell?"

"Some sort of paint or solvent or something."

"Oh, it's probably coming from the living room. I've been working in there... stripping off old wallpaper and removing the paint from the ceiling molding." She offered him a tentative smile. "I guess I've gotten so used to it I don't smell it anymore."

He grunted. "About meals. Janet didn't tell me what sort of arrangements she'd made with you. I imagine I'll be eating most of the time over at her place, but I'm sure there will be times when I'm not."

"Oh..." She looked surprised. "Actually, Janet and I really didn't discuss it, but you're welcome to eat here with us anytime. I always make breakfast. You'd be on your own for lunch, then I usually cook dinner around five."

He looked over at the pot on the stove. "If that's what you usually cook for breakfast, maybe I'll just skip that particular meal." He knew he was being unreasonably rude, but she looked far too appealing for his peace of mind.

Color flooded her face. "Oatmeal is Rachel's favorite breakfast, and it's quite good if it's eaten when it's first cooked. Of course, if it's not what you're accustomed to, I suggest you find a convenient restaurant or by all means skip it altogether." Her tone was the temperature of an iceberg, but Nick found a certain comfort in her coolness, preferring it to the crazy impulse he had to reach out and discover if her hair was really as soft as it looked.

"I think what I'll do now is go back to bed and try to get the rest of my sleep that was interrupted," Nick said, setting his cup in the sink. "And if I need a wake-up call, I'll be sure to leave word with your daughter." With those words, he turned and headed up the stairs.

Violet watched him go, a curious mixture of emotions racing through her. The man was an arrogant oaf! How was she ever going to survive him living upstairs in her house for the next six weeks?

Nick Elliot was like nothing she had expected. For some reason she'd expected someone considerably older, somebody less intense. All the times that Janet had spoken of her brother, the highly successful, prominent divorce lawyer, Violet had just assumed he was older, more distinguished, sort of an F. Lee Bailey type.

But Nick couldn't be much older than thirty-five, and he had the kind of dark good looks that had instantly made Violet feel ill at ease.

A small smile lifted the corners of her lips as she thought of the expression that had been on his face when she'd entered his bedroom. A giggle escaped her as she wondered what must have been going through his mind to awaken and have a little girl throw glitter on his head.

Her smile slowly faded as she thought of something else...the way his bare chest had looked with the early-morning sun emphasizing the muscular tone and firm planes. She shoved these thoughts aside. The man might look terrific in the early-morning light beneath a set of pristine sheets, but he sure didn't score any points in the personality department. She couldn't wait to talk to Janet. Janet hadn't mentioned anything about her brother's rudeness when she'd asked Violet to rent him the room.

In any event, she didn't have time to waste thinking about her rude, obnoxious boarder. Thank goodness he would only be here for six weeks. In the meantime, she had to shower and dress for her appointment with Mrs. Kevin Bodine. If she was lucky, she would come away from the appointment with the job of wallpapering and painting the Bodine dining room.

It was nearly five o'clock that evening when Violet finally left the Bodine mansion and hurried to get Rachel. Every day after school, Rachel went to Violet's mother's house for several hours. It was an arrangement that had worked well, cementing the relationship between grandparent and child, and allowing Violet the peace of mind in knowing Rachel was well looked after on the days Violet had to work.

She pulled up before her mother's small house, as always a smile tugging her lips upward as she saw the profusion of spring flowers that lined the sidewalk to the porch, the ceramic gnomes who peeked around the flowers, looking impish and more than just a little bit real.

As she walked up the sidewalk the dozen sets of wind chimes that hung from the porch eaves twin-

kled melodically. Her mother was more than just a
little bit eccentric, but she had a heart of gold and
a belief in the goodness of people and life.

"Hello?" she called as she walked in the front
door.

"In the kitchen," her mother returned gaily.

"Mmm, what's cooking?" Violet asked, stepping into the kitchen where the air was fragrant
with the scent of cinnamon and spices.

"We're baking a pixie pie," Rachel announced,
reaching out to give her mom a hug.

"It smells wonderful," Violet said, kissing her
daughter on the end of her flour-covered nose.

Violet's mother, Doris, smiled as she finished
crimping the pie crust, then set the pie into the
oven. "This is a very special pie, just for our fairy
friends. Rachel has a big favor she wants to ask the
pixies, so we thought we'd cook them up a pixie pie
and they'd be more agreeable." She wiped her
hands on a dish towel and motioned for Violet to
have a seat at the table. "I made a pot of tea just a
few minutes ago. Take a load off and share it with
me."

Violet sat down and smiled at her daughter.
"Rachel, why don't you run into the bathroom and
wash your face and hands real good. With all that
flour on your face, somebody might mistake you
for a pixie pie."

Rachel giggled and disappeared into the bathroom. Violet waited until she was gone, then she looked at her mother. "Mom, I think this pixie business is getting out of hand. Not only is she regularly sprinkling glitter on all the neighborhood animals, she's started throwing it on people."

"Humph, there are some people in your neighborhood who need to be sprinkled with magic dust," Doris exclaimed, pouring two cups of tea and joining Violet at the table. "Oh, quit frowning. You worry too much. All she wants is to make everyone happy. When Rachel doesn't need the magic anymore, she'll give it up. Sooner or later she'll outgrow it, but right now she needs it. Did you get the Bodine job?" she asked blithely.

Violet grinned at her, knowing she was changing the subject on purpose. "Yes, I did. It's going to be a lot of work, but the pay is terrific. I figure I should be able to catch up on all the bills and buy the wallpaper I've been wanting for my living room."

"You should just sell that monstrosity of a house and move into something a little cozier and less expensive," her mother replied.

"I can't do that," Violet protested immediately. "That house was Bill's dream house . . . our dream house. I can't sell it." She paused a moment and sipped her tea. "I figure if I do a good job on Mrs.

Bodine's place, then she'll tell her friends and before long I'll have more jobs than I know what to do with and money will no longer be a problem."

Her mother ran a hand through her short red hair, her blue eyes gazing at Violet worriedly. "You'll work yourself to death on that house."

"I'm entering the Homes League contest this year."

"But that's just a couple weeks away," Doris protested. "How are you ever going to finish up your house before then?"

Violet shrugged. "It's almost two months away, and I'll get everything done," she said determinedly, thinking about the contest. Each year the Homes League held a contest for the best restoration of the year. It had been Bill's dream that their home would one day be on the list of homes that had won the contest.

Doris gave Violet a sly look. "What's this I hear about you having a man in your upstairs?"

Violet smiled. "I suppose Rachel mentioned him. It's Janet's brother. He's here for six weeks on vacation. Janet asked me if I'd rent him my upstairs room. She didn't want him in an impersonal motel room, and apparently he refused to stay with her and Joe and the boys. It's really no big deal, just a way to do a favor for Janet and earn a little extra money."

"Is this the lawyer brother she mentioned to me the other day in the store?" Violet nodded. "Hmm, what's he like?"

"Mother, now don't you be getting that look in your eyes," Violet threatened.

"What look?" she asked innocently.

"That matchmaker look that always means trouble for me."

"Oh, nonsense, I was just being curious," her mother replied. "But I was looking into my crystal ball the other day and I did see that a man would be entering your life...a man who would become very important to you."

"Well, believe me, it definitely isn't Nick Elliot," Violet exclaimed. "He might be a great attorney, but he's definitely not my type. He's very...surly."

"All clean," Rachel announced, coming out of the bathroom and showing her hands to her mother.

"Okay, kiss Mimi goodbye and we'd better get home." Violet rose from the table. She watched as Rachel threw her arms around Doris's neck.

"Goodbye, Mimi, and don't forget to put the pixie pie out for the pixies. It's really important."

"Don't you worry, sweetpea. I'll set it out," Doris assured her, kissing Rachel soundly on her cheek. She also got up from the table and walked with Violet and Rachel to the front door.

"We'll see you tomorrow," Violet said, kissing her mother on the cheek. "Thanks."

"Don't forget, Mimi," Rachel said one last time as they walked out the door.

"What exactly is it that's so important that you're asking the pixies for?" Violet asked moments later as they drove home.

"I can't tell you. It's a secret. But it's really important and it's something I want more than anything else in the whole wide world," Rachel replied fervently.

Violet looked at her daughter for a moment, then sighed. Somehow she suddenly felt as if she were losing control of her life. She had a mother who baked pixie pies, a daughter with secrets and there was a man she didn't think she liked living in her upstairs.

She was relieved when she got home and there was no sign of Nick, who'd apparently gone over to his sister's house next door.

That's just fine with me, she thought as she made grilled-cheese sandwiches for her and Rachel's dinner. She wasn't ready for another dose of his particular brand of rudeness.

It wasn't until after dinner and Rachel's bedtime that Violet was able to get busy stripping the paint off the ceiling molding in the living room. She climbed up on the ladder, put on her protective goggles, then used a wire brush to dislodge chips of the green paint that covered the intricately carved molding.

Bill would have been so proud of the progress she'd made on the house. The third floor, where Nick was staying, was finished, the bedroom and connecting bath done in shades of green and brown. The second floor, where Rachel and Violet's bedrooms were, was also completed. The woodwork had all been redone, the walls papered in pleasing Victorian patterns.

Now if she could just get this living room finished in the next couple of weeks, then the house would be complete. Of course, she didn't want to think about the fact that sooner or later a new furnace was a must, and eventually the plumbing and wiring would need to be updated. Where the money would come from for these things, she had no idea.

She applied her steel brush to the ceiling with a vengeance.

Nick stepped out of Janet's house and breathed a sigh of relief. He loved his sister dearly, but it didn't take long for him to be completely overwhelmed by the noise, the chaos of her family. With three young boys and two dogs, there never seemed to be a quiet moment.

He stood for a moment, listening to the hush of the night surrounding him. Other than the musical notes of insects, there was a peaceful tranquility. It was quite a contrast to the night sounds he was accustomed to in his downtown Chicago high-rise apartment.

He looked over to the house next door, Violet's house, where the porch light illuminated the ornate gingerbread of the porch.

Violet...he felt a small niggling guilt at his rudeness with her. He'd spent the entire evening listening to his sister extol Violet's virtues, telling him what a good friend and neighbor she was, how difficult her life had been since her husband's death a little over a year ago, how hard she worked to keep body and soul together.

It wasn't Violet's fault that she hadn't been what he'd imagined when Janet had first told him about her. What did matter was that she'd been kind enough to help Janet out and let him rent the room upstairs.

As a divorce lawyer, he'd had to work closely with hundreds of attractive, sometimes desperately emotionally needy women, and he'd always managed to maintain a healthy distance. He was adept at being friendly and charming, yet maintaining control and keeping separate the part of himself he never gave away. He was confident he could do the same with Violet.

Besides, it would certainly be more pleasant for the next six weeks if he and Violet were on friendly terms. With this thought in mind, he crossed the lawn that separated the two houses and went into Violet's.

Hearing a strange noise coming from the living room he stepped through the threshold, instantly seeing Violet. She stood on a ladder, her back to him, one arm up over her head as she scraped the paint off the ornate ceiling molding.

As she worked the wire brush against the wood, her jean-clad bottom wiggled provocatively. For a moment Nick stood silently, almost mesmerized by the sight. He must have unconsciously made some sort of noise, for she gasped suddenly and twirled around. Her eyes widened behind the glass of the ridiculous goggles she wore.

"Oh, you startled me. I didn't hear you come in," she said, removing the goggles and descending the ladder.

"I'm sorry...I didn't mean to scare you," he apologized, noting again the beauty of her violet-colored eyes, the pale attractiveness of her shoulder-length hair. Remembering his resolve to be friendly, he offered her a tentative smile. "Looks

like somebody had bad taste,'' he observed, pointing to the pea-green paint she was in the process of
stripping off.

''The people who owned the house before we
bought it,'' she answered, her voice cool, but not
completely unfriendly.

''Looks like you have quite a job ahead of you.''

She nodded, not contributing anything to ease
the strain of the conversation. Apparently he'd
made her angrier than he'd thought with his rudeness of the morning. ''Well, I guess I'll just head up
to my room,'' he said, offering her another smile.
''Good night.''

''Good night,'' Violet replied, watching him as
he climbed the stairs and disappeared from sight.
She breathed a sigh of relief when he was gone.

She sank down onto the sheet-covered sofa, surprised by the effect his smile had on her. It had
lightened his features, crinkled the corners of his
bright blue eyes, made him look far too attractive.

When she had first considered renting the room
upstairs for extra money, she had thought it would
be nice to rent it to an old man, perhaps a retired
professor. A man who would enjoy being a surro-
gate grandfather to Rachel and a friend and men-
tor to Violet. She hadn't quite made up her mind
about renting the room when Janet had asked her
about renting it to Nick. Wanting to do something

special for Janet, who'd been such a support in the past year, and realizing the extra money would be a godsend, Violet had agreed to let her brother have the room.

Still, she hadn't expected him to be so...so male. In her wildest imagination she hadn't considered renting to a man who looked like Nick Elliot. When he'd smiled at her, her stomach had done a curious flip-flop and she suddenly had a horrid feeling that this whole arrangement was a terrible mistake.

Chapter Two

Violet and Rachel walked into the house, greeted by the scent of rich tomato sauce and garlic. Violet moved into the kitchen, surprised to see Nick standing in front of the stove, adding spaghetti to a huge pot of boiling water.

"What . . . what are you doing?" she asked.

Nick whirled around and smiled. "Ah, good, you're home. I wasn't sure what time to expect you. The spaghetti should be ready in about fifteen minutes."

"Oh, boy, bisghetti," Rachel exclaimed in delight. It was one of her favorite foods right up there with French fries and chocolate ice cream.

"Why don't you kick off your shoes and relax. There's wine in the fridge," he instructed.

She stared at him. She hadn't seen him since the night before when he'd come in from Janet's. All had been quiet from the upstairs that morning when she had left for her work at the Bodine place. "What exactly are you doing?" She repeated her original question.

"I believe I'm cooking spaghetti," he answered. "I just hope I didn't use too much garlic and not enough basil. It's been so long since I've had the time to make a pot of homemade sauce. I'm not sure I remember the exact measurements." He turned back around to stir the boiling pasta.

"That's not exactly what I meant," she replied, feeling as if she'd walked into the wrong house. "Why are you cooking?"

"Consider it my penance for my foul mood yesterday morning." He turned back around and threw her an apologetic smile. "I was tired and cranky and I'm afraid I took it out on you."

"You really didn't have to go to all this trouble," she said, moving over to the refrigerator and grabbing the bottle of wine. "A simple apology would have sufficed." She poured herself a glass of wine and sat down at the table. "I'm sure I owe you some money for the groceries you must have

bought to make this meal. I know I didn't have all
the ingredients you needed."

"Don't worry about it," he replied, dumping the
boiled spaghetti noodles into a colander in the sink.

"But that isn't fair. You're paying me a generous rent," she protested. "You shouldn't have to
buy groceries, as well."

"You might consider it generous rent, but compared to what I pay in Chicago, this is a real steal."
He dumped the pasta back into a bowl and ladled
sauce on the top. "You'd better tell your daughter
to wash her hands. This is ready."

Dinner was delicious. The pasta was cooked to
perfection, the sauce rich and spicy. The garlic
bread was warm and crusty and the salad fresh and
crisp.

Thankfully Rachel kept up a steady stream of
chatter, alleviating the need for Violet to make
conversation. Rachel told them about her day at
school, her friends, her favorite subjects.

As the little girl talked, Violet found herself
studying the man across from her. It was obvious
that he and Janet shared the same parents.

They both had the same rich, dark hair and blue
eyes that sparked with intelligence and humor. The
only difference was Janet's always radiated a welcomed warmth, while Nick's held a distance.

Still, with his Roman nose and the slight cleft in his chin, there was no denying that he was attractive. And when he smiled, it was easy to understand his success as a divorce lawyer. She couldn't imagine a judge anywhere, especially a female one, who wouldn't be swayed by his powerful, charismatic smile.

He'd looked as equally at home cooking in the kitchen as she assumed he did in the courtroom. That was the mark of a man confident in himself, the ability to look at home wherever he was, whatever he did.

"Mom told Mimi that you were surely." Rachel's words suddenly penetrated Violet's thoughts.

"Surely? Surely what?" Nick asked curiously.

Violet felt a warm flush sweep up her neck, covering her face. "Uh ... I think she means surly," Violet admitted softly.

"Ah ..." Nick grinned and reached for another slice of the garlic bread. "Yes, I was definitely cranky, but I'm much better now."

"It was my pixie dust that made you uncranky," Rachel announced proudly, her mouth decorated with the spaghetti sauce.

Violet handed her a napkin. "Wipe," she instructed.

Rachel wiped her mouth, her gaze still on Nick. "Do you know where pixies live?" she asked him.

"In pixie houses?" Nick guessed, amused indulgence softening his features.

Rachel nodded. "They live in houses made of spider legs and cats' eyes and the roofs are bat wings painted with moonlight. Mimi says the pixies like to play tricks but if you're nice to them, then they make your special wishes come true."

"Mimi?" Nick raised a dark eyebrow.

"My mother," Violet explained.

Rachel nodded. "Me and Mimi baked a pixie pie today. Mimi is going to set it out for the pixies and then they'll make my wish come true."

"It must be a very special wish to warrant a whole pixie pie," Nick observed.

"Oh, it is." Rachel nodded her head solemnly. "It's a secret wish, but it's the bestest one in the whole wide world." She smiled fully at Nick, exposing a missing front tooth. "Will you make bisghetti tomorrow night, too?" she asked hopefully.

"Rachel, honey, I'm sure Nick has more important things to do with his time than cook you spaghetti every night," Violet interjected.

"Actually, I was thinking of pizza tomorrow night." He laughed as Rachel clapped her approval. "That is if your mother doesn't mind granting me kitchen privileges." He looked at Violet. "I really do enjoy cooking. I find it very relaxing. In the last couple of years I haven't had time to indulge myself in the kitchen. Would you mind if I took over dinner preparations?''

Violet shrugged helplessly. Who was she to look a gift horse in the mouth? Besides, he'd already seen the disarray in her kitchen cabinets, so she had nothing left to hide in that area.

"Great." He smiled at Rachel once again. "Then it's pizza tomorrow night."

"Pepperoni?" Rachel ventured with beguiling eyes.

"Sure, why not?" he agreed amicably.

Violet watched this exchange with interest, surprised by how easily Rachel seemed to accept Nick. The little girl had always been rather shy and withdrawn around strangers, particularly male ones. But there wasn't a hint of her usual shyness with Nick. It was strange ... very strange how comfortable she appeared to be with Nick.

"You have a very unusual daughter," he observed a few minutes later as he and Violet cleaned up the dirty dishes.

"Yes, she's pretty special," Violet said, running a sink full of sudsy hot water.

"She sure looks a lot like you," Nick added, bringing the last of the dishes from the kitchen table to the countertop next to the sink.

"That's just a lucky coincidence."

"A coincidence?" Nick looked at her curiously.

"Rachel is adopted," Violet explained. "My husband, Bill, couldn't have any children so we adopted. We got lucky when they matched us up with Rachel."

"I'd say she got pretty lucky, too." He grabbed a dish towel and started drying the dishes Violet had washed.

"Please . . . you don't have to do that," she protested. "You did all the cooking. That was more than enough."

"Nonsense. With me drying and you washing, the cleanup will just take a few minutes." He picked up a glass from the dish drainer and twirled it against the absorbent towel. "Why don't you have an electric dishwasher? I thought every woman in America had one."

Violet shrugged. "I don't for several reasons. Mostly because it would jar the old-fashioned flavor of the kitchen. Besides, I've always rather enjoyed washing dishes by hand."

What she didn't tell him was that this was always a time when she and Bill enjoyed the intimacy of the mundane household chore. Violet would wash and Bill would dry and while they did, they shared the events of their days with each other.

In the past year Violet had grown accustomed to the solitude. She used her dish-washing time to evaluate the day gone by and anticipate the morning to come.

It was strange, perhaps a little frightening how pleasant it was to once again be sharing this moment of the day with a male. She hadn't before realized how lonely she was around this particular hour.

She also hadn't noticed just how broad Nick's shoulders were. But now, as he stood right next to her, she felt as if he were taking up all the space in the kitchen. His body not only emitted an inviting warmth, but a pleasantly masculine woodsy scent, as well. He'd rolled up his shirtsleeves, exposing well-shaped forearms covered with dark, curly hair.

She felt a distantly familiar coil of heat in the pit of her stomach, the spark of an emotion long suppressed.

She breathed a sigh of relief as she finished washing the last pan. It suddenly seemed important that she move away from him, step back from his body heat and provocative scent.

She walked over to the stove and wiped its surface with a sponge, concentrating more than usual on removing every splatter. "Actually, I'm surprised you aren't at Janet's tonight. I figured she wouldn't let you out of her sight."

"I had lunch with her and Joe today. The boys had baseball games tonight so I told her I'd just hang out here for the evening and see them all to-morrow. Would you mind if I made a short pot of coffee?'' he asked.

"Not at all. I usually drink a cup after supper,'' she said agreeably, feeling more in control as the strange heat inside her dissipated. ''Why don't you go relax in the living room and I'll bring the coffee out when it's ready.'' She relaxed completely as he nodded his head, prepared the coffee and ambled out of the kitchen.

As she waited for the coffee to drip through the machine, she contemplated the man who had cooked their meal. The charming, smiling Nick who'd greeted her this evening was a far cry from the surly man she'd met yesterday. Somehow she liked the rude Nick Elliot better. For some reason, he was less threatening.

She leaned onto the counter, surprised by her own assessment of the charming, attractive Nick as a threat. Yet she knew she was vulnerable. She'd finally gotten over the shock of Bill's sudden heart attack, and her grief had eased over the passing year since his death. She had learned to accept the loss and now found herself lonely, more than a little ready to accept the possibility of a new relationship.

But of course, she'd be a complete fool to get involved with Nick Elliot. In spite of his charming veneer, she suspected he was a man who gave very little of himself to anyone. Besides, he was only going to be here for six weeks, then he would fly back to his high-powered, stressful life in Chicago. "Besides, I'm not even sure I like the man," she muttered to herself, fixing a tray to carry into the living room.

Nick felt Rachel's gaze on him as he wandered around the living room. She sat on the sheet-covered sofa, her legs swinging to and fro to the beat of the music emanating from the videotaped, animated program on the television.

He ignored her, instead looking at the ceiling molding where Violet was in the process of stripping off the disgusting pea-colored paint and refinishing it back to its natural mahogany beauty.

What a job, he marveled, noting the intricately carved scrollwork in each corner. She'd already completed the work on two walls, and was half-finished with the third. Three of the walls had been stripped of their wallpaper, and the paper on the fourth wall hung in shreds.

He tried to imagine what the room would look like when all the work was completed and the furniture was no longer covered with sheets, but Nick had little imagination and he couldn't see beyond the mess.

He sat down on the other end of the sofa. He looked at Rachel, who stared at him, obviously finding him much more interesting than the cartoons on the television set. "Didn't your mother ever tell you it's rude to stare?" he asked her.

She shook her head, her fair hair flying out from her face like angel's wings. She smiled at him, a sweet, tentative grin. "You have a dent in your chin," she observed. Nick reached up and touched the cleft in his chin self-consciously. "Mimi says dents are where fairies kissed you. I have one here. See..." She smiled widely, pointing to her cheek where a deep dimple appeared.

She scooted over to sit directly next to him and lightly touched the cleft in his chin. Her hand was small and dainty and she smelled of sunshine and innocence.

"Here we go," Violet said, entering the room with the tray of coffee.

"Look, Mommy, Mr. Nick has a fairy kiss. Mommy has two on her bottom," Rachel announced, causing Nick to choke and Violet's face to flame brightly.

"Uh... here's your coffee," Violet said, setting the tray down on the table, her gaze not meeting his.

"Thanks," he returned, unable to hide the grin that stretched across his face. He reached for a cup and took a sip, schooling his features into neutrality.

"You've got quite a job ahead of you in here," he said, gesturing to the work. "Why didn't you take down the molding to refinish? Wouldn't it have been easier to work on that way rather than working over your head?"

"Yes, it would have been much easier," she agreed. "But the molding is so old and the wood dry. I was afraid that in trying to get it down I would destroy it."

He nodded. "Janet told me you do this kind of work for a living."

Violet smiled. "I'm trying. Although so far the jobs have been few and far between." Her smile widened. "But I just got a really good one doing a living room for one of the most prominent women in Glenville. I'm hoping good things will come out of it."

She sat down on the chair across from him. He could smell her from where he sat, a pleasant floral scent he'd noticed as they'd eaten. He took another sip of his coffee, trying to ignore the almost physical effect she had on him. He jumped as a knock fell on the front door.

"Now who can that be?" she asked, getting up to answer it.

A moment later, a red-haired woman in a voluminous purple-flowered caftan walked into the living room. No, that wasn't right, Nick amended. She didn't walk in, she sailed in, her caftan flapping like wind-whipped canvas on a fast-moving boat.

"Mimi!" Rachel greeted the woman, jumping off the sofa and launching herself at the older woman. *Mimi* ... Nick realized that this must be Violet's mother. As he eyed the older woman, he saw the physical similarities in the shape of the eyes, the uptilted nose, the generous smile that curved her lips.

"Hello, sweetpea," she exclaimed, giving Rachel an affectionate hug. "I just thought I'd drop by and visit for a little while." She eyed Nick with sharp, intelligent blue eyes. "I'm Doris Heely, Violet's mother. And you must be Janet's brother, Nick." Nick rose from the sofa as she held out her hand to him. "Sit back down," she ordered after shaking his hand. "Oh, I see you made coffee," she said to Violet. "I'd love a cup." She floated down onto the sofa next to Nick, enveloping him in her floral scent. Rachel immediately snuggled up next to her.

"I'll just go get another cup," Violet murmured, disappearing into the kitchen.

"I understand you're from Chicago," Doris said.

"Yes, I—"

"Nice city," she continued. "I was there a couple years ago for a big psychic fair. It was marvelous, I had a dozen readings done. Of course, Chicago is much too big, much too fast for the likes of me. I much prefer it here in Glenville where the pace is slower and everyone knows everyone else. Do you believe in reincarnation?"

Nick looked at her blankly, having difficulty following the course of her conversation. He was vaguely aware of Violet coming back into the room with a third coffee cup. "Uh...well, I'm not—"

"I thought so," Doris exclaimed knowingly. "I knew when I shook your hand that you were a nonbeliever. Vibrations...they give you away every time. But that's all right," she assured him with a bright smile. "Not everyone is illuminated with the vision of truth."

"Here you go, Mother." Violet handed her the cup of coffee, then sat down in the chair across from the sofa.

"You know, I was just telling Paul the other day that it's a shame more people don't understand and accept the idea of a continuation of life after death."

"Paul? Is that your husband?" Nick managed to interject the question as Doris paused for breath.

"It depends in which lifetime you're talking about. I think he was my father in one and my sister in another. But in the most recent lifetime we shared, he was my lover." She played with the gold chain around her neck, at the end dangled a small crystal. She released a wistful sigh. "Poor Paul, we just can't seem to figure out how he got stuck in the spiritual world."

"You mean this Paul is a ghost?" Nick stared first at Doris, then at Violet.

"The ghost of Paul Revere," Violet explained, her lavender eyes imploring him not to laugh. "He lives in Mother's attic."

"I can tell you don't believe this, either," Doris said, leaning over and patting Nick's knee. "It's all right. I don't expect everyone to believe. Even Violet has trouble sometimes."

"I believe," Rachel said, looking up at her grandmother with loving eyes.

"Of course you do, darling." Doris smiled at the little girl fondly. "But that's because you are one of the special ones. Cheers," she said to Violet and Nick, lifting her cup to her mouth and sipping her coffee. "Ah, wonderful. Violet does make a good cup of coffee, doesn't she?"

"Actually, Nick made the coffee," Violet explained. "He also cooked spaghetti for dinner."

"Ah, a man who cooks!" Doris patted his knee once again. "Violet's daddy loved to cook—didn't do much else, God rest his soul. Still, he could make a mean New England pot roast." She waved her hands as if to dismiss the topic and turned her bright gaze to Nick. "So, how do you like our fair town?"

"Mother, Nick's only been here for two days. He's scarcely had time to look around."

"You must take him to the museum," Doris said. "The Dillon Glenville museum. I'm sure you'd find it quite interesting. Dillon was the founder of Glenville and the museum is full of fascinating artifacts." Doris shivered. "We've held several successful séances there and the vibes from the other world are just magnificent."

Nick wanted to ask her who they contacted in séances if everyone was reincarnated, but he bit back the question, instinctively knowing he couldn't win a logical debate with somebody who had Paul Revere living in her attic.

"How do you like your room?" Doris asked. "I thought Violet did a wonderful job on it. The duck wallpaper was my idea."

"It's very nice," Nick agreed. He was very pleased with the spacious bedroom and connecting bath.

"You being here for six weeks is a perfect chance for Violet to see if she wants to rent the third floor permanently," Doris explained. "I told her to think carefully before letting a stranger in the house." She beamed at Nick. "But of course, you aren't a stranger. Janet's practically family and that makes you family, too."

They all jumped as a knock came at the door. "What now?" Violet asked, getting up to answer. She opened the door to see Mr. Richardson, her neighbor, glaring at her.

"Let me talk to her," he growled without preamble.

"Who?" Violet asked, although she knew perfectly well who he was talking about.

"That mother of yours, that's who," the old man exclaimed.

"Andrew Richardson, what in the world are you blathering about?" Doris joined them at the door and Violet saw that Rachel and Nick were right behind her.

"You know what I'm blathering about... the same thing I always blather about when you come over here. You parked that car of yours right in front of my driveway. You're blocking it." He glared at Doris, who glared right back.

"What difference does it make? You don't even drive a car anymore," she returned, her cheeks flaming an attractive shade of pink.

"It's my driveway and I want that car of yours moved right now!" He banged his cane on the porch to emphasize his point.

"I swear, Andrew, you're the most sour man I've ever met in my life," Doris retorted. "I just know that in a previous life you must have been a lemon!"

"I don't want a previous life, thank you very much," the older man exclaimed. "I'm having enough problems living this one."

"Perhaps if you smiled once in a while, life would be a little more kind to you," Doris returned haughtily.

"And you..." Mr. Richardson glared at Violet. "That daughter of yours is still sprinkling that glitter on my poor Mr. Peabody."

"It's not glitter, it's pixie dust," Rachel said, peeking out from behind Doris.

"Whatever it is, it doesn't belong on my cat," Mr. Richardson said.

"You could use a dose of pixie dust yourself, you old poop," Doris muttered. "As it so happens, I was just getting ready to leave so I'll be glad to move my car from your driveway." She turned and smiled at Rachel. "Why don't you walk out with

me, sweetheart. The pixies left something special
for you this afternoon.''

"Pixies . . . bah," Mr. Richardson said in disgust. ''Just move that car.''

"Good night, Violet. Nick, it was wonderful
meeting you.'' She smiled serenely at both of them,
then turned and glared at Mr. Richardson once
again. ''I'll move my car all right. Not because you
told me to, but because I'm ready to go home.''

She and Rachel brushed past the old man, who
followed behind them, grumbling and muttering
beneath his breath. Nick watched them go, his mind
trying to assess the evening he'd just had.

He needed to talk to his sister. He must have
done something terrible to Janet when they were
kids, something that had her holding a grudge.
That was the only explanation as to why she had
rented him a room in an insane asylum.

Chapter Three

Nick peeked around the corner of the staircase, anticipating a sneak attack from the little glitter princess. In the past three days, Rachel had taken on the dimensions of a miniature guerrilla fighter, lurking in shadows, hiding behind curtains... intent on achieving the goal of dusting him with glitter as often as possible. And it was no longer silver. For the past three days Rachel had been flinging red glitter on him whenever the opportunity presented itself. He hadn't told Violet, finding it beneath his dignity to tattle on a six-year-old.

Seeing no sign of the impish minx, Nick headed for the back door. Since the night he'd met Violet's mother, he'd done his best to keep a low profile, unsure if he wanted to fraternize with a family that included a grandmother who carried on conversations with Paul Revere, and a little girl who believed in pixies. Although Violet appeared relatively *normal,* who knew what crazy eccentricities he'd discover if he took the time to know her better.

He walked out into the backyard, breathing deeply of the sweet spring air. It was Saturday and all around him he could hear the sounds of people working in their yards. The roar of a lawn mower, the high-pitched whine of a weed-eater, the rhythmic thud of someone chopping a tree. The sounds filled him with the desire to get his hands dirty.

There had been a time when he'd loved yard work, but that had been in another lifetime. His high-rise apartment in downtown Chicago afforded him little opportunity to indulge his penchant for working outdoors.

He looked around, noting the tall grass in the yard, the flower bed that needed to be cleaned out, the rose vines that had grown awry from the white-painted wooden trellis. Surely Violet wouldn't mind if he did a little yard work.

He headed for the detached garage, grunting in satisfaction as he found an antique-looking, pull-start lawn mower, a rake and a shovel.

For the past several years there had been no time for anything but work, satisfying his need for professional success, but starving his soul's desire for relaxation. This vacation was a much-needed rest for his brain and a chance to enjoy the simple things in life.

With a powerful yank of the cord, the mower roared to life. After the first few minutes of mowing, he pulled off his T-shirt, allowing the warm sun to heat the bareness of his back and chest. As he pushed the mower, his thoughts turned to Violet.

He'd seen very little of her the past couple of days. In the mornings she was usually gone by the time he got out of bed, and she didn't return until suppertime. They small-talked over the evening meal, discussing nothing more personal than the weather or Rachel's day at school. Most evenings immediately after eating, Nick went to Janet's to visit with her family. When he returned he went directly to his room and to bed.

He knew Violet worked long into the night. Although he never heard her, each morning he saw the results of her nightly diligence. The ceiling molding was now nearly stripped. The job was getting finished, but he didn't understand why she worked into the wee hours of the night. What forces drove her to maintain such a schedule?

He grinned and swiped his brow with the back of his hand. Perhaps Violet's odd work hours were one of the eccentricities of her personality. Probably one of the more benign, he thought wryly.

Knowing Violet's mother, Violet probably practiced meditation and levitation and slept in a bed with an energy-producing pyramid over it. Hmm, now that thought produced some interesting possibilities. He shook his head, dismissing thoughts of the attractive blonde with her pale purple eyes.

Violet dropped the heavy bags of groceries onto the kitchen table and heaved a deep sigh. She looked at her watch and grimaced, as always amazed how mundane errands could eat up the precious hours of a day. It was nearly noon and Rachel would be home by two. She had been invited to a friend's house down the street to play for several hours and Violet had taken the opportunity to take some clothing to the cleaners, buy stamps at the post office and pick up two bags full of groceries.

She had hoped to have some time to get some work done in the living room, but the day was shaping up with too many things to do and too little time. Oh, well, she'd just have to work twice as long tomorrow. The deadline for the Homes

League contest was looming large, a scant six weeks away and the living room was far from being ready.

She shoved the meat items into the freezer, keeping out a package of hot dogs. It was such a nice day. Hot dogs out on the grill, a crock of baked beans and macaroni salad would make a perfect evening meal.

For the past three nights Nick had cooked, sumptuous meals that would have Violet and Rachel spoiled when he went back to his life in Chicago. At thoughts of her upstairs boarder, she paused, listening intently for any sound of movement from above her. She heard nothing. He was probably still asleep. She had no idea what time he got out of bed as he was always still there when she left for work in the mornings.

A smile curved her lips upward as she thought of her boarder. If the next one she got was as nondemanding as Nick, it would be great. In fact, in the past couple of days she'd seen very little of him. He seemed to be making a conscious effort to keep out of her hair. And that suited her just fine.

She moved away from the refrigerator and carried the bag of canned goods to the pantry. She put the canned goods away, then walked back across the kitchen, pausing at the window as her gaze was captured by movement. Nick. He was fighting with the rose trellis, trying to get the errant vines to climb and cling to the wood.

She smiled as she watched his efforts, the frustration that lined his face as he wrestled with the tenacious vines. Her smile slowly faded. He was shirtless, his broad back glistening in the midday sun. His jeans were tight, clinging to his well-shaped buttocks and legs. As he worked, the muscles of his back jumped and danced provocatively, provoking in Violet the sudden shocking image of the feel of those muscles, sun-warmed and hard beneath her fingertips. Heat suddenly exploded in the pit of her stomach and she moved away from the window, wondering if it was possible to suffer menopausal heat flashes at the age of thirty.

She'd just finished putting the last of the groceries away when the back door opened and Nick walked into the kitchen, bringing with him the evocative scent of freshly mowed grass, sweet-scented flowers and sunshine.

"Whew, it's getting hot out there," he said in greeting, grabbing a glass out of the cabinet and filling it with cold water from the pitcher in the refrigerator.

Violet stepped back, overwhelmed by his overt physical maleness, surprised by her reaction to it. "You're supposed to be on vacation. You shouldn't be doing my yard work," she chided, wishing desperately he'd put his shirt back on and cover up the gorgeous expanse of chest.

"For the past five years all I've done is sit at a desk or in a courtroom doing mind work. Believe me, working in the yard is definitely a welcomed change." He grinned and tilted the water glass up to his lips.

Violet watched in fascination as he drank deeply, a droplet of water escaping his lips, rolling down his chin, down the expanse of his throat and stopping on his chest, where it seemed to sizzle and evaporate against the heat of his flesh.

"Uh . . . I've got some cleaning to do upstairs," she muttered, needing to escape the small confines of the kitchen, confines that seemed to grow smaller by the second.

She raced up the stairs as if trying to outrun the crazy, outrageous thoughts that steamed in her head. Funny, it had been a very long time since she'd felt the stirring of sexual desire for any man. Since Bill's death she hadn't entertained a single sexual thought. So why did the sight of Nick's bare chest and well-shaped, jean-clad bottom create a barrage of erotic visions in her head?

"What you need is to scrub a bathtub," she muttered, grabbing onto the physical task that always seemed to focus her thoughts in the right direction. She went into the bathroom that she and

Rachel shared and liberally sprinkled cleanser into the tub.

As she worked, she thought about sex. It had never been high on the list of priorities between Violet and her husband. Theirs had been a relationship built solidly on friendship, companionship and mutual intellectual interest. Comfortable...yes, that's how things had been with Bill.

But the thoughts she entertained about Nick made her feel distinctly uncomfortable. She shoved her troubling thoughts aside, renewing her efforts at scrubbing away the bathtub ring.

The rest of the afternoon flew by. Violet cleaned with a frenzy while Nick puttered in the backyard. It wasn't until she went outside to light the barbecue grill that he put away the tools and went upstairs to shower.

"Thanks for all the work you did today," Violet said later as they sat at the kitchen table eating hot dogs. "The yard looks better than it has in months."

Nick shrugged. "I enjoyed it. It was much too nice a day to spend it napping or reading. Besides, it felt good to be using brawn instead of brain power."

"What does that mean?" Rachel asked curiously.

He grinned at her. "It means I used my muscles to work today."

"Do you have big muscles like Popeye?"

"No, nobody has muscles quite like Popeye." He laughed.

Rachel scooted out of her chair and moved to stand right next to him. "Let me see," she prompted, gesturing for him to bend his arm and flex.

Nick hesitated a moment, then did as she bid him, causing his arm muscle to pump up beneath his short T-shirt sleeve.

Rachel's eyes widened in awe as she ran her hand over it. "I'll bet it's almost as big as Popeye's." She turned to Violet. "Here, Mommy, you feel it."

"Rachel, we're trying to eat dinner," Violet exclaimed, feeling a blush steal over her face.

"Come on, feel how big it is," Rachel implored. Nick grinned helplessly at Violet, who sighed impatiently and leaned over and ran her hand over his flexed muscle. She immediately withdrew her hand, shocked by the inviting warmth of his flesh.

"It's a very nice muscle. Now sit down and finish your dinner," she told her daughter.

Rachel did as she was told and Nick focused his attention on his plate of food, surprised at how the touch of Violet's hand on his arm had affected him. Although her touch had been soft, a mere whisper of fingertips across his skin, the effect had been immediate and electric.

He now gazed at her surreptitiously, noting the high color of her cheeks, the way she studiously avoided looking at him.

She really was beautiful, with her pale hair and delicate features. If he allowed himself, it would be very easy to be attracted to her. But he didn't intend to allow himself. He'd only be here for a couple of weeks. He'd have to be completely crazy to get involved with her, and Nick prided himself on his self-control and sanity.

"Are you coming to the carnival with us tonight?" Rachel asked him, interrupting his thoughts.

"Carnival?"

"Rachel's school is having a carnival this evening," Violet explained. "It's really not a big deal...just a small-town sort of thing."

"Sounds like fun," Nick observed. "*Would* you mind if I tagged along with you?" What possible harm could there be in going with them to a school carnival? he thought. Janet and her family had already told him they had plans for the evening and a carnival would be better than spending the evening all alone up in his room.

"You're welcome to join us," Violet returned.

Immediately after eating and doing the dishes, the three of them took off walking toward Rachel's elementary school.

The evening air was pungent with the scent of approaching summer. The sweet smell of flowers, rich earth and green grass all combined to produce a heady, pleasing odor.

They walked in silence for a few minutes, Rachel skipping ahead a few steps then pausing for the adults to catch up with her.

Dusk had begun to fall, painting the western sky in vivid shades of orange and pink, casting a golden light that surrounded them.

Nick noticed that each house they passed was well kept, the yards neatly tended. Here and there people sat on front porches, waving and calling greetings as the three passed.

"I have yet to see a house that needs painting," Nick observed after they'd walked two blocks.

"We're one of the few small towns who have managed to maintain a large sense of community pride." Violet smiled at him and he noticed the way the twilight loved her features, coloring her ivory skin a pale gold and lighting her hair with luminous flames. Her jeans hugged her slender legs to perfection and the pink blouse she wore did little to hide her shapely breasts.

He refocused his attention to their surroundings, uncomfortable with his observations of Violet's attractiveness.

"Rachel, wait a minute. Hold my hand," Violet instructed as they approached an intersection.

Rachel grabbed Violet's hand, then held out a hand to Nick expectantly. "Mommy says to always hold hands crossing the street," she said.

"That's a good thing to do," Nick agreed, taking Rachel's small hand in his. As she gripped his tightly, he experienced a strange heart flutter. Probably indigestion from the hot dogs, he reasoned, relieved when they reached the other side of the street and Rachel skipped on ahead.

As the one-story brick school came into view, new sounds wafted on the evening breeze. Music and laughter rode on the air, as if inviting all of those in the vicinity to come and enjoy the carnival. As Rachel danced ahead of them in eager excitement, Nick felt a growing sense of anticipation. He grinned inwardly. His social calendar had been pretty dismal the past couple of days. That could be the only explanation for his anticipation over a small-town school carnival.

"Oh, Mommy, look! Pony rides!" Rachel squealed, pointing toward the school playground where an area had been roped off and two Shetland ponies were giving rides to wiggling, giggling kids. "Can I have a ride? Please, Mommy? Please?"

Violet laughed as Rachel jumped up and down. "Yes, you can have a pony ride. Run and get in line and I'll buy you a ticket." She laughed again as Rachel's little legs did double time until she was in the line of other children waiting for rides. "She'll probably be sick from too much excitement by the end of the night," Violet said as she and Nick approached the ticket booth.

"That's the best kind of sick to be," Nick returned. "I have a feeling I might be rather sick by the end of the night."

Violet looked at him in surprise. "Why?"

"I smell cotton candy, and I have absolutely no willpower when it comes to the stuff." He grinned boyishly and Violet couldn't help but compare the way he looked at this moment to the way he had looked and acted on the first morning she'd met him. A couple of days of sleep and relaxation had transformed him from a surly grouch to a pleasant person whose smile was contagious. Or perhaps it was Rachel's pixie dust that had done the trick, she thought with an inward grin.

"I can see why Janet loves living here," he observed minutes later after Rachel had finished her pony ride and they were wandering around the school gymnasium looking at the various booths that had been set up. "Everyone is so friendly."

"People aren't friendly in Chicago?" she asked curiously.

"It's a different kind of friendliness. Less personal."

Violet nodded. "I personally can't imagine living anywhere else but here. This is the sort of town that embraces you, makes you feel as if you're part of a big, extended family."

"You don't have any other family?" Nick asked.

She shook her head. "It's just Rachel, Mom and me. That's why your sister has been so important to us. She's like a sister to me and a favorite aunt to Rachel."

Nick smiled. "Yeah, Janet is great. She's into all this stuff... small town, kids, the importance of family."

Something in the way he said it made Violet think these were things he was not into, but before she had a chance to ask him anything, Rachel came running up to them, her face shining with excitement.

"Mommy, there's Grandma!" Rachel exclaimed, pointing across the room where Violet's mother sat at a card table, with a sign advertising Fortunes Told hanging above her head. She was clad in a black caftan painted with silver stars and half moons.

Violet groaned beneath her breath as Doris spied them and stood up, motioning them over.

"Violet, dear, I've been looking for you all evening, and Nick, how nice of you to come to this little soiree." She gestured to the chairs in front of the table. "Sit down, sit down. I'd love to read your palm, Nick."

He hesitated a moment then slid into the seat across from Doris, laying his hand palm up for her to see.

"Oh, no, you don't," Doris protested. "It will cost you one dollar to know the secrets of the future." She smiled apologetically. "It's for charity, you see."

Nick nodded good-naturedly and pulled a wrinkled dollar bill from his jeans pocket. He set it on the table, then replaced his hand, palm side up in front of her.

In the blink of an eye the dollar disappeared into Doris's cash box, then she took Nick's hand in hers, a wrinkle furrowing her brow as she studied the lines that crisscrossed his palm. "Interesting..." she said, casting a sly look at Violet, then back at Nick. "Ah, yes, you are a hard case...pragmatic to a fault. You don't believe in anything you can't see, ignore half of what you feel." Doris smiled slyly.

"But I see changes ahead. Big changes that will shake you to your very core, make you rethink your values and what's important to you." Her sly grin widened. "I see love in your future."

Nick tried to contain his snort of disbelief, but it escaped despite his efforts.

Doris seemed unaffected by his show of skepticism. "That's right, laugh, but you can't hide from the magic of the pixies." Doris's eyes twinkled knowingly and her large gold earrings danced wildly from her ears.

"Mom, I'm sure Nick finds this all fascinating, but we have lots of other things to see and do." Violet decided to take pity on Nick and free him from her mother's prophecies.

"Run along, then," Doris agreed, smiling benignly at them.

"Your mother is quite unusual," Nick said as they walked away from her table.

"She's a wonderful, loving person," Violet returned defensively, then flushed. "Sorry, I didn't mean to snap at you. I get defensive because there are some people in town who laugh at her, and she's a beautiful person inside. I know she's different. She's one of a kind, that's for sure. She's wonderful with Rachel, and her heart is solid gold."

"Mommy, I see the fishing booth.... Can I go fish?" Rachel tugged impatiently on Violet's hand.

Violet smiled down at her daughter, grateful for the change of subject. "I think fishing is just what we need. We'll see who catches a bigger one—you, Nick or me."

"You're on." Nick laughed enthusiastically.

None of them were able to catch one of the fat trout and from there they made the rounds of all the booths, throwing darts, tossing basketballs, admiring handcrafted items and gorging themselves on circus peanuts and cotton candy. Both Rachel and Violet groaned when Nick bought his third cotton candy. He just laughed at their looks of dismay.

It was nearly ten o'clock when Violet saw that Rachel was wilting, her eyelids droopy even as she protested that she wasn't a bit tired.

"Time for home," Violet said, overriding Rachel's cranky protests. She picked the little girl up in her arms as she and Nick started out of the gymnasium.

"Here, let me take her," Nick said, reaching out to take Rachel out of Violet's arms.

"No, it's all right. I'm used to carrying her," Violet protested, obviously surprised when Rachel held her arms out to Nick.

"I want Nick to carry me," the little girl exclaimed. "Carry me, Nick," she appealed.

Nick took her from Violet, Rachel's slender arms wrapping firmly around his neck, her soft breath whispering against his cheek.

Strange emotions welled up inside Nick's chest. He'd never held a child before, had never felt the trusting way they clung, had never smelled the scent of innocence that emanated from them. It was a strange feeling, one that sent pleasant warmth cascading through him.

He knew the moment she fell asleep, and he marveled at how easily she'd given in, as if confident she'd be safe in his arms.

They walked in silence, the moon overhead a fat sliver of pie that cast down pale silvery illumination. Crickets chirped a merry rhythm and somehow Nick felt as if indeed, the town did wrap itself around him, embracing him in welcoming arms of warmth.

He looked over at Violet, noting that the brilliant moonlight lovingly caressed her. She'd laughed a lot over the past couple of hours, and her laughter had been contagious. Her eyes had sparkled with her humor and her lips had entranced him as they'd curved upward in generous smiles. For a single moment he'd wondered how they would taste. Sweet . . . yes, they would definitely be sweet. He quickly shoved that thought away.

Rachel sighed, as if in the middle of a pleasant childish dream, and Nick fought his impulse to reach out and grab Violet's hand. There was something frightening in this whole scene, he thought warily. It was much too intimate, much too provocative...threatening in a strange sort of way. To somebody peering out of one of the houses they passed, they probably looked like a family, but it was just a facade. Nick knew better than anyone that families fought, people separated, kids were ripped emotionally and used as innocent pawns. He didn't want any part of it. Love...marriage...they were merely illusions that had nothing to do with reality.

As Violet's house came into view, he sighed in relief, anxious now to escape this woman and child who had managed to somehow touch his heart in a place where it had never been touched before.

In a few more weeks he'd be back in Chicago, back to life in the fast lane, dealing with couples who had begun life together with promises of love forever, and ended it with bitterness and anger. There was a certain amount of comfort in this knowledge.

"I'll take her now," Violet said as she unlocked the front door and they walked into the silent, darkened house.

Nick shook his head. "It's all right. I'll carry her on up to bed." He tightened his arm around the sleeping child.

Violet led him up the stairs to the little bedroom where a menagerie of stuffed animals greeted them, lined up neatly on the pink-ruffled bedspread. As Nick waited, Violet quickly scooted the toys onto the floor, then turned down the covers. She then removed Rachel's shoes and socks.

It wasn't until Nick gently laid Rachel on the bed and pulled the sheet up around her that she opened her eyes and smiled at him. She reached out a hand and moved it softly across his cheek in a caress. The gentleness of her hand, the sweetness radiating from her sleepy blue eyes caused a strange pain to well up inside Nick's chest. "Good night, Nick," she breathed. Then her hand fell away and her eyes closed once again.

"Good night," he muttered gruffly, then with a curt nod to Violet, he escaped to his room.

Chapter Four

"Did you have a good time last night?" Doris asked Violet the next morning.

Violet looked down at her mother from her perch on the ladder. "Sure, the carnival was lots of fun."

"I noticed you seemed to be laughing a lot. Nick—he was laughing lots, too." Doris ran a hand through her short red hair and smiled as if intensely pleased by some knowledge only she possessed.

Violet set her wire brush down and sighed. "So what's your point, Mom?"

"Oh, no particular point," Doris protested with a wave of her hands. "I was just making a casual observation. The three of you looked nice together . . . like you fit.''

Violet sighed again, this time with a wealth of exasperation. ''Mother, Nick is a boarder, nothing more, nothing less. Don't go trying to make something out of nothing.'' Violet renewed her efforts, applying the wire brush to the ornate corner ceiling molding with a vigor.

''My goodness, you're certainly in a persnickety mood,'' Doris returned, rising off the sofa as Rachel skipped into the room.

''I'm all ready, Mimi,'' Rachel exclaimed.

''Then we're off on our adventure,'' Doris said enthusiastically. Their adventure was a trip to a museum in Cleveland.

Violet climbed down off the ladder and gave Rachel a kiss. ''You be good for Mimi and don't go wandering away from her in the museum,'' she instructed.

''I won't,'' Rachel promised.

''We should be back by suppertime,'' Doris said as they walked to the front door.

''I was planning on throwing some burgers on the grill for dinner. Why don't you plan on staying and eating with us?'' Violet suggested.

''That's a wonderful idea,'' Doris exclaimed, then frowned. ''If you're going to cook out, you might just as well invite that old coot from next door over."

"You mean Mr. Richardson?" Violet looked at her mother incredulously.

Doris's face flushed slightly. "If you don't invite him, I'm sure he'll just complain about the smoke and will glare out his window and make us all miserable. Besides, the old fool probably hasn't had a decent meal since his wife died two years ago."

"Okay, I'll ask him, but I doubt if he'll come," Violet agreed reluctantly. She watched as the two got into Doris's car, then waved until it had disappeared from sight.

Once they were gone, she crawled back up on the ladder and began working once again. As she scraped, her thoughts drifted back to the night before.

Yes, she'd had a good time. She'd had more fun than she could remember having in a long time. Nick had been enthusiastic, wanting to try his hand at every booth. He'd been friendly with the people there, charming the old ladies running the craft booths and teasing Rachel's little friends good-naturedly. His laughter had rung out in the gymnasium often, sending tingles of pleasure racing up and down Violet's spine.

On the way home, there had been a quiet intimacy in sharing the nighttime walk with him. Seeing Rachel sleeping in his arms had made her heart stir, made a warmth suffuse her that had kept away the chill of the night air.

She hadn't thought of the void left in Rachel's life when Bill had passed away. The little girl needed a man to relate to, a daddy. But Nick Elliot definitely wasn't a good bet for that role.

The strange intimacy on the walk home the night before had lasted only moments. She'd sensed the minute he'd distanced himself, his jaw hardening, his body stiffening in silent protest. She didn't know what had happened, but the moment he'd muttered good-night and run to his own room, Violet had seen the look in his eyes, and it had been pure fear.

Then this morning he had stumbled into the kitchen, grabbed a quick cup of coffee, then escaped to Janet's house where he'd been all morning.

She quickly dismissed him from her thoughts. It was ridiculous to waste valuable time thinking about a man who'd be out of their life in a few weeks. In the meantime she had a lot of work to complete before the contest. She'd been putting in such long hours at Mrs. Bodine's, her own room renovation was moving much too slowly.

For the rest of the afternoon she worked with a vengeance, scraping, puttying, sanding and varnishing. She took a break at noon, only long enough to grab a quick peanut butter and jelly sandwich and run next door to ask Mr. Richardson if he'd like to join them for dinner. To her surprise, after a moment of hesitation, the old man agreed.

She stopped working and put her tools away at three o'clock. She made a tossed salad and cut up potatoes for frying later, then hurried upstairs to the shower.

As she stood beneath the hot spray of water, thoughts of Nick once again intruded. She had to admit it, she was attracted to him. It was crazy, it was insane, but it was there. There was something about him that stirred her, made her think of languid mornings beneath cool, crisp sheets, moonlit nights of kisses and caresses. The memory of his laughter, so deep, so utterly masculine, produced a longing inside her. She was ready to share laughter again. She was ready to love again.

She sighed impatiently and grabbed the bar of soap, scrubbing at her face and hair as if she could scrub the nutty thoughts right out of her head.

She had a very clear vision of what she wanted out of her life. She wanted Rachel happy and well adjusted. She wanted her business to thrive. She

wanted to follow through on Bill's dream and get
the house in the Homes League contest. None of
her plans included a burned-out lawyer who lived
in Chicago.

Nick came in the back door, immediately hearing the sound of the shower running someplace
upstairs. He could smell the scent of fresh varnish
and knew Violet must have spent the day working
on the living room.

He sat down at the kitchen table, enjoying the
quiet after the chaos of Janet's place. He loved his
sister dearly, but as a bachelor he wasn't accustomed to the noise level that her dogs, the three
boys and all their friends could generate.

Violet's house was quieter, much more welcoming. He frowned at this thought, somehow disturbed by its implications. In fact, he'd been
somewhat disturbed ever since the walk home from
the school carnival the night before.

At some point during that short walk from the
school to Violet's house, he'd experienced a brief
moment of self-awareness, a single second when
he'd seen and recognized the solitary path he'd
chosen for himself.

But it had been an intelligent choice, he reasoned. For years he'd watched people destroying
each other, fighting over important issues such as

finances and child-rearing practices, and inane things such as brands of toothpastes and sleeping habits.

Yes, he'd definitely made the correct decision when he'd chosen his solitary path. But in spite of knowing the rightness of his choice of life-style, he couldn't control the evocative image of Violet that flashed in his mind.

As he listened to the sound of the shower overhead, he envisioned her standing beneath a spray of water, her pale hair wet, her lavender eyes framed by starry bursts of water-darkened lashes. In his mind's vision he could see her slender shoulders all soft and soapy. He could easily imagine the rounded curves of her breasts, her skin all slick and sweet-smelling. The visions sent a wave of heat through him. Intense and unexpected, the heat expanded outward, engulfing him in invisible flames.

He looked up, startled as Violet came into the kitchen, bringing with her the provocative scent of minty soap, clean shampoo and a light floral perfume. He flushed, realizing he'd been so caught up in his imaginings, he hadn't noticed that the shower had stopped running. He only hoped she wasn't a mind reader, or that his face didn't reflect the X-rated thoughts he'd just entertained about her.

"Oh, you're back," she exclaimed, obviously as startled by his presence as he was at hers.

"I figure six hours of Janet's particular brand of noisy family life is all any man can handle," he returned, pleased that his voice sounded normal. "And I've also decided Joe should be up for sainthood," he finished, referring to Janet's quiet, stoic husband.

Violet laughed, pouring oil in a skillet on the stove. "Joe's terrific, and Janet's household might be noisy, but it's the noise of love."

Nick merely shook his head, watching as she poured the potato slices into the hot oil. "Is there anything I can do to help?" he asked as she grabbed an onion and began chopping it. Her jean-clad bottom wiggled with each slice of the knife and Nick pulled his gaze away from the enticing sight.

"You could light the charcoal in the barbecue. I've invited Mom and Mr. Richardson over for hamburgers." She smiled at Nick's look of disbelief. "I know, it's crazy, but inviting Mr. Richardson was Mom's idea. I was surprised he agreed to come over."

"He's probably afraid he'll miss a good opportunity to complain," Nick returned. "Rachel should be sprinkling him with bucketfuls of her pixie dust."

Violet smiled. "I think Mr. Richardson is beyond a pixie-dust fix."

Nick stood up from the table. "I'll get the grill going. I don't want him to complain because we had to wait for the coals to be ready."

As he filled the grill with charcoal and squirted it liberally with starter fluid, he thought of the evening to come. A beautiful woman, an impish child, a neighborhood grouch and a metaphysical nut... should make for an interesting night.

"Make sure you cook that burger real good. I like mine well-done," Mr. Richardson said, peering over Nick's shoulder as he flipped the meat patties.

"He means he wants it black and crusty, like his heart," Doris interjected, blithely smiling as the old man glared at her.

"Look, Mr. Richardson, Nick has a fairy kiss in his chin," Rachel said, pointing to the cleft in Nick's chin. "Do you have any pixie kisses on you?"

"Pixie kisses, bah. I suppose that's a bunch of nonsense your grandmother taught you," Mr. Richardson exclaimed. "Crazy woman always did have a head full of nonsense."

Doris walked over and placed an arm around Rachel's shoulder. "No, honey. Andrew doesn't have any pixie kisses. He quit believing in magic a long time ago."

"Crazy woman," Mr. Richardson repeated as Doris and Rachel went into the house to help Violet.

"Have you known her for a long time?" Nick asked curiously.

Andrew nodded. "She and my wife were close friends for years, although since Irene died two years ago, I don't see Doris very often." He frowned, his grizzly eyebrows meeting in the center of his forehead. "Just often enough to give me a constant case of heartburn." He looked over to where the three females were now setting plates on the picnic table. "I'll say one thing for her... she's a feisty old girl."

Nick was surprised to hear a small note of admiration in the old man's voice. So, that was the way it was, he mused. Beneath the flames of antagonism were sparks of attraction. He shook his head ruefully. It would seem love could make fools out of anyone, regardless of their age.

"That done enough for you?" He gestured to the hamburger in the middle of the grill, well-cooked and nearly black.

"It'll do," Andrew grunted, moving over to the picnic table and sitting down.

Within minutes they were all seated at the table, eating their fill of the hamburgers, fried potatoes, corn on the cob and tossed green salad. As they ate,

Rachel told them about her day with Doris at the museum, enthusiastically describing the displays they'd seen. "They had all kinds of big stuffed animals. And they had this big room full of dinosaurs," Rachel explained. "I liked the brontosaurus. They were so big and scary-looking, but they just ate plants."

"My personal favorite is the creatopsians... the ones who looked like rhinoceroses but had huge bony plates and long pointy horns," Andrew said, for the first time joining in the conversation.

"We saw those!" Rachel exclaimed in delight. "Do you know about dinosaurs?" she asked the old man.

"It takes one to know one," Doris said beneath her breath.

Andrew ignored her and shrugged. "A little. I have some books at home about the giant creatures." He looked at Rachel assessingly. "I suppose if you were really careful, I'd let you borrow them for a couple of days. 'Course, I don't want to get them back with any chocolate-covered pages or sprinkled with that glitter of yours," he warned.

"I'd be very careful," Rachel answered solemnly, her blue eyes earnest.

Andrew merely grunted and returned his attention to his food.

As they finished eating, the conversation shifted to the town fair that would take place in a couple of weeks' time.

"The Baskin sisters are going to sing all afternoon from the bandstand," Doris exclaimed. "And the mayor and town council is providing the burgers and hot dogs."

"Humph, those women sound like frogs croaking, and the council members should be providing better garbage service," Andrew mumbled.

"Oh, honestly, Andrew," Doris expelled a huff of exasperation. "Can't you ever say anything nice about anything or anyone?"

"I like that red dye that you put on your hair," Andrew retorted, causing Doris to open, then close her mouth speechlessly. Nick grinned inwardly, amazed that anything or anyone could render Doris speechless.

After dinner, Rachel and Doris played catch with a bright red ball while Violet cleaned off the table, insisting she didn't want any help. Andrew and Nick sat in lawn chairs, each drinking a cold can of beer.

Dusk was falling, the evening air intensifying the smell of the grass, the flowers, the sun-baked earth. The laughter of Rachel and Doris rang out, mingling with the muted sounds of dishes rattling from the kitchen. Nick leaned back, took a deep drink of his beer, then sighed in contentment.

It was strange really, how little he missed his job and his high-rise apartment in Chicago. He'd obviously needed a vacation much more than he'd thought.

Surely after another week or two of this tranquil existence, he'd grow hungry to be back home, back in the drama of the courtroom, back to the city he loved. But for the time being, he felt a kind of contentment he hadn't experienced for a very long time.

Darkness had begun to fall when Violet stepped out on the back patio. "Rachel, come on, peanut, it's time for bed." Rachel threw the ball to her grandmother one last time, then joined Violet on the porch.

"I guess I'd better get back home, too. This night air makes my bones hurt." With the aide of his cane, Andrew eased himself up and out of his chair.

"Mr. Richardson, what about the books you promised I could borrow?" Rachel asked.

The old man frowned. "Come on, Andrew," Doris said, taking his arm. "I'll walk over to your place and get the books for the child." She smiled at Rachel. "You can look at them tomorrow after school at my house." Before Andrew had a chance to protest, Doris guided him across the yard and toward his house.

"Good night, Nick," Rachel called as Violet led her into the house.

"Good night, pixie princess," he returned, leaning back once again in his chair, reluctant to call an end to the evening.

He tipped his head back, watching as the stars overhead seemed to magically appear as the darkness of the night deepened. God, it had been forever since he'd seen stars. Back home the lights of the city obliterated the twinkling gems. When he'd been a young boy, he'd enjoyed stargazing, but looking at the stars, smelling the roses along with all other leisure-time pursuits had been left behind when he'd gotten old enough to get his priorities in order.

Nick straightened up in his chair as Violet came back outside, sitting down in the lawn chair next to his. "I think she was asleep before her head even touched the pillow."

Nick smiled. "She had a busy day with the trip to the museum."

"Every day is a busy one when you're six years old. There's so much to explore, so much to learn, so many adventures to complete." Violet leaned back in her chair and released a sigh that mirrored the one Nick had released only moments before.

For a few minutes they sat in a companionable silence. Once again Nick found himself admiring the way the moonlight loved Violet. It seemed to seek out and highlight each and every delicate feature. He could smell her light fragrance, felt as if it surrounded him. She looked very pretty this evening, clad in a pair of white slacks and a red floral print blouse that emphasized her slenderness but didn't diminish her curves. He had yet to see her when she looked anything less than attractive.

"It's nice out here, isn't it?" she said softly.

"Beautiful," he agreed, noticing that all around them night insects manufactured their own special brand of music.

"I've always loved the night—there's something mystical about the darkness of nighttime."

Mystical? He looked at her dubiously. Here it comes, he thought, the eccentricities she's been hiding. She's probably going to tell me she turns into a werewolf and bays at full moons.

She smiled, as if aware of where his thoughts were heading. "Don't worry," she assured him with a small ring of laughter. "I'm only my mother's daughter up to a point. All I mean is that there's a feel about the darkness, like the whole world becomes smaller, more intimate."

Nick nodded, surprised to realize he knew exactly what she meant. "In Chicago, the night does the exact opposite. It makes you feel like the world is a huge place. You feel isolated and...alone." He bit off the last word, surprised that another adjective had jumped into his mind. Lonely... Strange, he'd never thought of himself as lonely before. "But of course, I love Chicago, and I love my work there," he added, banishing the unsettling thoughts from his mind.

"Do you miss your work?" she asked curiously.

"Strangely enough, so far I don't. I think I was more burned-out than I realized. I've worked very hard for the past several years without a vacation."

"What made you decide to take a vacation now?"

Nick smiled reflectively. "One day, several weeks ago, I was in the courtroom representing a client in a particularly nasty divorce. The husband and wife were screaming, totally out of control. The judge was banging his gavel for order, and all I could think about was a fishing pole."

"A fishing pole? Do you like to fish?"

Nick laughed. "No, I abhor it. As far as I'm concerned, there's nothing more boring. But the image of a fishing pole wouldn't go away. Then I realized it wasn't the act of fishing that I wanted, rather it was what a pole signified. Peace, tranquility... sitting on a shoreline and watching the world go by. It was then I realized I desperately needed a vacation."

"Why here? Why choose Glenville?"

Nick shrugged. "Why not? Janet was here, and she's been bugging me for years to come out and visit with her."

Violet smiled ruefully. "There's certainly not much recreation here."

"Not true," he protested. "Just think, I've already enjoyed a school carnival and a barbecue with two of the most colorful characters this town has to offer." Violet laughed, and once again Nick realized he liked the sound of her laughter.

"Speaking of colorful characters...I wonder what's taking mother so long." She looked over to the house next door. "Poor Andrew, she's probably reading his palm or regressing him back to learn about his previous lives." She laughed and Nick again wondered what her lips would taste like. Would they be sweet and soft, or hot and demanding?

"What about you?" he asked, refusing to dwell on the subject of the condition of her lips. "What do you do for recreation besides attend school carnivals and throw barbecues?"

She was silent for a moment or two. "When my husband was alive, we did lots of things. We went on picnics, took yearly vacations to Yellowstone and the Grand Canyon. Since his death, there hasn't been time for much recreation.'' There was no self-pity in her tone, only a simple statement of facts.

"It must be difficult, trying to keep up with this big house and taking care of Rachel all alone," he observed.

"Rachel is the easy part. All I have to do is love her and she pretty well takes care of herself. The house is a lot of work, but it was so important to Bill...to both of us." Her voice was soft, reflective and as she spoke, her gaze was on the moon overhead. "Bill was an architect and the moment he saw this house he fell in love with it. He knew it would require a lot of work, a lot of money, but it was going to be our dream house when we completed it. He didn't see the work involved, he saw possibilities. Eventually, I'll still get it finished." She looked at him, her eyes glowing a deep purple. "What about you? No shared dreams with a special woman?"

"I have my own dreams. I've never met anyone I particularly wanted to share them with."

"Too bad," Violet said. "Sharing dreams is part of the wonder of being in love."

Nick shook his head, a wry grin curving his lips. "Ah, yes...love." He paused a moment. "I don't believe in it."

Violet looked at him in shock. "You don't believe in love?"

He shook his head. "It's my belief that there's no such thing. After working in divorce court for the last five years, I've decided it's just a pretty word people dream up to justify desire or sate loneliness. It has nothing to do with reality."

"Surely you don't really believe that," she protested, shocked at the cynicism in his voice, somehow saddened if he truly believed his words.

"Yes, I do. Love...marriage...I've seen the aftermath and it's not a pretty sight." He shook his head. "Even my own parents divorced when I was fifteen. Love can't go the distance. Somebody always walks away." He looked at her, his eyes certain and knowing. "No, I don't believe in love." His voice was firm with conviction, making Violet shake her head in wonder.

"Ah, a true, hard-nosed cynic." She laughed uncertainly and stood up. She touched his arm lightly. "We'll just have to see what we can do to change that." With these words she murmured good-night and disappeared into the house.

Nick watched her go, wondering what in the hell she'd meant by her words. They'd sounded almost like a challenge. He frowned, wondering why he suddenly felt extremely nervous.

Chapter Five

"Now, what did you mean by that?" Violet asked herself minutes later as she turned down the blankets on her bed. Why on earth should she care if Nick Elliot was a hard-boiled cynic who didn't believe in love? She shouldn't care... but for some reason she did.

For some inexplicable reason, despite Nick's testimony to the happiness of his life back in Chicago, Violet sensed a hard core of loneliness deep within him. She had a feeling that despite his protests to the contrary, he had a yearning to be with somebody, a need for more than just himself. It was easy for her to see it, for she related to it, had felt the same pangs of loneliness within herself.

So what happens now? she thought, crawling beneath the sheet and shutting off her bedside lamp. She was lonely; he was lonely—but fate had been unkind to cast together two people whose lives could never intersect for an indefinite period of time.

He was only here on vacation, and she couldn't risk her heart, her peace of mind to a relationship that would be fleeting at best. *Just my luck,* she thought ruefully, *to be attracted to a man who's only going to be here for a few weeks and doesn't believe in love.* She'd be a complete fool to get involved with him at all. She closed her eyes, a small smile touching her lips. Still . . . it would be nice if she could get him to believe in just a little bit of magic.

Over the next couple of days, she didn't have to worry about getting involved with Nick in any way. She spent her days working at the Bodine house and he spent the evenings next door at his sister's.

Friday night as Violet got ready for bed, her thoughts once again shifted to the cynical Nick. How sad to go through life and not realize the wonder and magic of love. How sad to never know the special connection that two people could have when their hearts were committed to each other.

It's not my problem, she told herself firmly, getting into bed and closing her eyes.

She awoke some time later, her heart beating frantically in response to whatever it had been that had jerked her from her dreams. She lay unmoving for a long moment...waiting...anticipating.

She had just about drifted back to sleep when a scream rent the air, a scream of complete terror coming from Rachel's room.

In a split second Violet was up and out of bed and running across the hallway. She flipped on the light, unsurprised to see that Rachel was in the middle of one of her nightmares. The little girl's eyes stared widely at some unseen horror in the corner, and her entire body shook with abject terror.

Violet moved quickly to the bed. She sat down and gathered the little girl into her arms, trying to still the uncontrollable trembling of her body. "Rachel...Rachel, baby, wake up. It's just a dream. Wake up."

"Monsters," Rachel gasped, coming awake but clinging to Violet in frantic terror. "They were going to get me. They were going to eat me. Please don't let them get me, Mommy. Please don't let them get me." She sobbed, hiding her face against the silky folds of Violet's nightgown.

"Shh," Violet crooned, stroking the little girl's slender back, whispering soothing words of nonsense. "I won't let anyone or anything get you.

You're safe." She held Rachel close, rocking back and forth in the ancient ritual of mothers everywhere.

"Is she all right?"

Violet jumped at the sound of the male voice, causing Rachel to cling to her even tighter. She looked up to see Nick standing in the doorway. It was obvious he had been pulled from sleep by Rachel's cries. His hair was wildly tousled, his chest bare and his jeans were half-buttoned, as if pulled on in haste.

Violet averted her gaze from him, finding the sight of him disconcerting. "She's fine," she answered. "Just a bad nightmare. She'll be okay now." In fact, Rachel's sobs had subsided to occasional hiccuping ones and her eyelids drooped in exhaustion. "It's all right now," Violet said to Rachel, tucking her back in beneath the covers, all too aware of Nick lingering in the hallway just outside the bedroom door. "All the monsters are gone now," she assured her daughter, planting a soft kiss on her forehead.

"Draw the monster circle, Mommy," Rachel said, her voice still holding a tinge of lingering fear. "Hurry and draw the monster circle."

Violet nodded and stood up. With the index finger of her right hand pointing, she walked around the edge of Rachel's bed. As she walked, she solemnly recited the rhyme that had given Rachel peace following each nightmare.

"Monster circle burning bright, keep monsters away throughout the night. Ghosts and goblins stay away, Rachel is safe 'til the light of day." She repeated the words like a magical chant. By the time she'd said them for the third time, Rachel was once again sound asleep. Violet gave her one last soft kiss on the forehead, then turned out the light and left the room.

"Will she be all right now?" Nick asked worriedly as Violet stepped out into the hallway.

Violet nodded. "She should sleep peacefully for the rest of the night."

Nick expelled a deep sigh and ran his hand through his tousled hair. "Whew, when she screamed like that, my heart stopped dead."

"I'm sorry, I should have warned you that she occasionally has nightmares," Violet apologized. "It's been a while since her last one and I just didn't think about telling you."

"Well, my adrenaline is jumping too fast for me to go back to sleep right away. How about if I fix us a cup of tea?" he asked.

Violet nodded, too weary to protest, yet knowing it would take her a little while to relax enough to go back to sleep once again.

Nick led her into the living room and pointed her to the sofa. "Why don't you sit down right there and I'll bring the tea in when it's ready."

As Nick disappeared into the kitchen, Violet sank down onto the sofa and leaned her head back, closing her eyes tiredly. She'd hoped Rachel's nightmares were gone. It had been nearly a month since the last one and she'd really begun to think that finally Rachel was secure and happy and wouldn't be bothered with her night terrors anymore. *But apparently I was too optimistic,* Violet told herself. Thank God for pixie dust and monster circles, it was the little bit of magic that Rachel needed so desperately.

In the kitchen, Nick placed the teakettle on the stove, thinking about the scene he'd just observed. There was something beautiful, something so touching in a mother soothing a child's fears. The picture of Rachel in Violet's arms, the two of them rocking back and forth, would remain in his mind for a very long time to come. Violet in her soft blue gown, Rachel in pale pink, their blond heads so close together... Something about the whole scene had made a heart connection with him.

He leaned against the counter, waiting for the water to boil. He'd spent the past couple of days distancing himself from Violet and Rachel, afraid of the feelings he was experiencing at this very moment.

He scoffed at his own nervousness, knowing he was being ridiculous. Anyone would have felt a twinge to their hearts had they seen the scene in the bedroom. There was nothing for him to be nervous about; it had nothing to do with him.

He jumped as the teakettle whistled shrilly.

It took him only minutes to prepare a tray. ''Here we go,'' he said as he came back into the living room carrying the tray that held two cups of tea, the sugar bowl, milk and lemon wedges. ''I wasn't sure how you like it,'' he explained, setting the tray on the coffee table and sitting down next to her.

''Just plain tea,'' she said, gratefully taking the cup he held out to her. She took a sip, then set the cup back down. She leaned her head back once again and expelled another sigh.

''You're working too hard,'' he observed, pausing to take a drink from his cup, then setting it back on the coffee table. Without conscious thought, he reached out and swept an errant strand of pale hair from her forehead. At his touch, her eyes flew open in surprise, their color reminding him of twin amethyst gems.

He'd had no intention of kissing her, but as she stared at him, her eyes seemed to hold a silent invitation. Her lips were moist and slightly parted and before he knew his own intentions, he leaned forward and touched them tentatively with his own.

Their heat surprised him. He'd somehow expected the sweetness, he'd anticipated the softness, but he hadn't expected the blazing inferno her lips offered his. And as he tasted them, he allowed all the reasons why he shouldn't be kissing her to fly away like ashes in the wind.

He wanted her. The knowledge hit him hard, surprised him with its intensity. He wondered vaguely when it was that he'd begun to desire her so intensely?

He deepened his kiss, evoking a moan from her and he realized she wanted him, as well. This knowledge stoked the fires of his desire even higher.

He wrapped his arms around her shoulders, enjoying the contrast of her cool, silky nightgown against his hands and the flaming heat of her mouth against his.

Leaning into her, he guided her down into the cushions of the sofa, covering her body with the length of his. As his hands moved across the silky softness of her shoulders, his lips trailed downward, tasting first the flesh of her sweetly scented neck, then lingering in the hollow of her throat.

She tasted so good, felt so wonderful in his arms. Her body fit comfortably against his, her breasts pressed intimately against his chest, their peaks rising up as if to fight against the constraints of the thin material that was between them. With a groan of frustration, he swept the flimsy nightgown straps down from her shoulders, pushing the bodice down to her waist.

Violet was lost in a maelstrom of sensations. In all the years of her marriage to Bill, she'd never experienced the height of passion she felt at this moment.

Bill's caresses had been satisfying, but not all-consuming. His kisses had been comfortable, not unrelenting, not tasting of the urgent hunger that marked Nick's. She had no defenses against the overwhelming demand of his mouth, the powerful sensations his caresses evoked within her.

She fought against the dizzying emotions, afraid of losing her rationale to the tumultuous aching Nick evoked in her. As his tongue lightly flicked at one of her nipples, she gasped, tangling her hands in the thickness of his hair, crying out his name both as a protest and a plea.

She moved her hands from the tangle of his hair to his back, reveling in the feel of taut muscles beneath smooth, heated flesh. She was lost . . . lost to the passion he stirred in her, helpless to fight against the sensual hunger of her own body.

She was aware of his arousal, conscious of his rapid breaths that warmed her already hot skin, the tautness of his body pressed so intimately against hers. Feeling the result of his desire for her, knowing how badly he desired her, only sent her reeling deeper into a haze of passion.

He raised his head and looked at her, his eyes pools of midnight blue flames. "Violet," he breathed, and kissed her again, an intimate exploration of lips and tongue that made her breathless. "I want you, Violet."

For a moment she stared at him blankly. Want...yes, Nick would accept the emotion of desire, she mused. The words caused rational thought to seep back into her passion-smoked brain. His words also forced her to remember what he'd told her before...that he didn't believe in love.

"Nick..." She pushed against his shoulders, at the same time pulling her nightgown back up. Her face flamed hotly as he sat up, obviously confused by her sudden protest.

He looked at her expectantly, his chest still rising and falling rapidly. Violet felt her blush deepen as she thought of how eagerly she had responded to him, how easily he'd been able to make her lose control and let things get out of hand.

"I'm sorry...I shouldn't have let things go so far," she said, emitting a shaky little laugh of embarrassment. "I apologize. Besides, I thought you told me the other night that you didn't believe in love.''

He shrugged. ''I don't, but that doesn't mean I don't believe in desire and sex.''

''Then we have a little problem,'' she said, standing up from the sofa. ''I don't want to have one without the other. You see, I don't just make love with my body, I do it with my heart, as well.'' She wrapped her arms around herself and smiled at him. ''Good night, Nick.''

He watched her go up the stairs, still able to taste the sweetness of her mouth, wanting once again to feel the warmth of her body pressed against his. He couldn't remember a time when he'd wanted a woman more than he wanted Violet at this very moment.

Love and sex...what did one have to do with the other? Making love and being in love were two totally separate concepts. She'd wanted him—he'd felt it in her kiss, seen it in the depths of her eyes. So why hadn't she followed through on her desire? And what on earth did her heart have to do with anything? It was all very confusing to him.

She confused him. She was a bundle of contradictions with her monster circles and magic. Yet she possessed a work ethic that had her putting in hours that daunted even him. Yes, she was an enigma.

He leaned his head back and closed his eyes. It was obvious that the kiss had been a mistake. What had ever prompted him to kiss her in the first place?

We're two healthy adults sharing a house, he rationalized. The middle-of-the-night setting, her in a flimsy nightgown—both were intimate and provocative. It was only natural that he would kiss her. Any sane man would have done the same if given the identical circumstances. Pleased with his assessment of the situation, he got up and headed for bed.

"Hi, Nick!"

Nick looked up from the flower bed where he'd been working to plant a row of petunias. He grinned at the sight of Rachel peeking her head out the second-story window. "Hey, munchkin, what's cooking?"

Rachel shrugged, then with a giggle, she threw a handful of red glitter out the window. Nick ducked, but not before the red mist rained down on his head.

"Rachel!" Violet stepped out onto the back porch just in time to see the crime being committed. Nick looked up, but the culprit had disappeared from sight.

"I'm sorry," Violet said, walking over to him as he stood up and shook his head. She motioned for him to bend his head down and she took her hands and raked them through the rich darkness, causing the red glitter to fall to the ground. "Red...? Now that's a switch. Usually it's silver," she murmured.

"She's been throwing red glitter for a while now," Nick commented, enjoying the sweet-smelling closeness of Violet's body, remembering how her hands had tangled in his hair the night before, how she'd moaned his name so breathlessly.

This was the first he'd seen of her all day. She'd already been gone by the time he'd gotten up that morning. Then she'd called him at noon to say that she'd be working late at Mrs. Bodine's and for him to go ahead and eat dinner without them.

"There," she said. "I think I got most of it." She pulled her hands out of his hair and stepped back, as if suddenly conscious of their intimate nearness. Her face flushed and Nick fought a sudden impulse to reach out and taste once again the sweetness of her luscious mouth.

"Well..." She took another step backward. "I guess I'll just get back to work inside."

"Why don't you sit down out here and enjoy the last of the beautiful evening?" he suggested. "Surely your work can wait for a little while. Besides," he added, kneeling back down by the flat of petunias waiting to be placed in the earth, "we he-men like to have women watch us while we work."

"This woman has work to do of her own," she said, smiling apologetically, then disappearing back into the house.

Nick set back to work, a curious frustration forcing his spade a little deeper as he turned over the soil and made holes for the plants. What was with the woman? Didn't she realize there was more to life than work? He smiled ruefully at these thoughts. That same sort of observation could have been made about him in the not-so-distant past.

Again he was struck by how odd it was that he didn't miss Chicago and his law practice at all. He was enjoying the time spent in this small town, where people greeted him on the streets with smiles of welcome and where there was a community friendliness that was absent in the bigger city.

He turned his head as he heard the back door slam and Rachel came out, her expression mournful. She sat down next to him on the ground and rested her chin in her palms. "I got in trouble," she explained.

"How come?" Nick asked innocently.

She raised her pale eyebrows and looked at him as if he were addle-brained. "You know," she replied.

"The pixie dust?"

She nodded. "Now I'm grounded for three whole days and can't see any of my friends." She sighed, a world-weary sigh that made Nick hide a grin. Still, three days of grounding seemed like cruel and unusual punishment for a six-year-old whose only crime was tossing out a little pixie dust.

"Maybe I could talk to your mom, get you an early parole," he said tentatively.

Rachel rewarded him with a brilliant smile. "Thanks," she said, then shook her head ruefully. "Boy, moms get mad over the silliest stuff."

"Maybe your mom doesn't think it's silly stuff," he observed. "Maybe she's worried that the glitter could get in somebody's eyes and really hurt them." Nick leaned back and eyed the little girl curiously. "Besides, what's the deal with the red glitter? How come you keep throwing it on me?"

Rachel studied her shoes, as if suddenly fascinated by the pink-striped laces. "I can't tell you," she finally answered. "It's a secret. I made a wish and the pixies won't make it come true if I tell you."

"Surely telling me won't ruin the secret."

Again Rachel gave him her are-you-dumb-or-what? look. "Pixie wishes are like birthday wishes. If you tell anyone, they won't come true."

"Oh." Nick picked up his spade and began working again, thinking that he had a lot to learn about pixies and wishes.

A silence grew between them, one that Nick found distinctly uncomfortable. He didn't know what to say to a little girl. He'd never spent any time at all around kids except Janet's boys, and all he had to do to begin a conversation with them was mention baseball or football. What did little girls like to talk about? "You want to help?" he finally asked, gesturing to the flower bed, desperate to break the silence.

"Sure," she agreed eagerly. "I like flowers," she said after a few minutes, her dirt-covered hands working to dig another hole.

"So do I," Nick agreed.

"And I like pizza," Rachel said after another minute.

"Hmm, it's one of my favorites."

Rachel looked extremely pleased. "And I love chocolate ice cream."

"At least two scoops."

"But I hate Jimmy Maxwell."

Nick looked at her in surprise. "Who's Jimmy Maxwell?"

"He's a boy in my class at school. He pulls my hair and scribbles on all my papers. And he eats bugs." She shivered, a delicate little tremor of disgust.

"Then I guess I hate him, too." Nick smiled as Rachel giggled.

For the next hour they worked side by side. By the time they finished with the flowers, darkness had started to fall.

"They look pretty, don't they?" Rachel said, admiring the colorful plants.

Nick nodded. "You did good work." He reached out and touched the end of her dirt-splattered nose. "Come on." He stood up and brushed off the seat of his pants. "We'd better get you inside. It's getting dark."

Rachel stood up and brushed off her jeans, imitating Nick's actions perfectly. She grinned up at him and offered her hand for him to clasp.

He hesitated for a moment, noting its grubby condition, then realizing his looked the same, he returned her grin and took her hand. Together they walked toward the house.

"I wonder what Mommy is doing? She never lets me stay out when it's this dark," Rachel observed.

"She's probably in the middle of scraping that ceiling and doesn't realize it's gotten so late."

"She's always working on this dumb old house," Rachel exclaimed. She looked up at Nick and smiled brightly. "I guess grown-ups just do silly stuff sometimes."

"I guess so," Nick said with a laugh. This from a little girl who threw glitter and believed in pixies.

They entered the kitchen, then walked into the living room, where Violet lay sound asleep on the sofa. "Shh," Nick whispered to Rachel. "Let her sleep," he instructed. "Why don't you run on upstairs and get ready for bed."

"Will you come and tuck me in?"

He nodded absently, his gaze lingering on the woman on the couch. As Rachel ran up the stairs, Nick moved over to where Violet slept.

She'd apparently just sat down for a moment to rest, but had drifted off into exhausted slumber. Her wire brush was still gripped in her hands, and the ridiculous goggles she wore when scraping paint were shoved up on her forehead.

Despite the pea-green paint chips in her blond hair, in spite of the smudge of dark shadows beneath her eyes, she looked beautiful.

He gently removed the brush from her hands, a wave of tenderness sweeping through him. He took the afghan from the back of the sofa and covered her up, his heart dancing wildly in his chest as she stirred, mumbled incoherently, then smiled in her sleep.

She must be having pleasant dreams, he thought, surprised to realize that he wished he could crawl right into her head and experience those dreams with her. What did women like Violet Sanders dream about? For some reason, he hoped she dreamed of him.

"Nick?"

He looked up to see Rachel standing on the stairs. She was clad in a pink cotton nightgown and he could tell from where he stood that her face and hands had been scrubbed clean. "Come tuck me in," she whispered, then scampered back up to her room.

With a lingering backward glance at Violet, he went upstairs to Rachel's room where he found her already in bed. He stood awkwardly next to the side of the bed, unsure what the correct procedure was for tucking in a child. "Uh . . . you want me to read you a story?"

She shook her head and motioned for him to sit on the edge of the mattress. "Mommy usually just talks to me for a little while."

Nick eased himself down next to her. "What sort of things do you usually talk about?"

Rachel shrugged her shoulders. "Just stuff."

"Princess, you have to help me out here. I haven't had much experience in these sort of things," Nick confessed.

Rachel studied him for a long moment, her blue eyes appraising. "Do you like my mommy?" she asked.

"Sure," Nick answered, slightly uncomfortable. "She's a real nice lady."

Rachel nodded in satisfaction. "Do you like little girls?"

"I don't know any."

Rachel clasped one hand over her mouth and giggled. "Silly Willy, you know me."

Nick looked at her in mock surprise. "Are you a little girl?" he asked incredulously. "All this time I thought you were a pixie princess."

Again Rachel giggled. "Not really. I'm just a little girl."

"Well, I like you, so I guess that means I like little girls." He was surprised to realize it was true.

She nodded in satisfaction. "And I think if little girls knew you . . . they'd like you, too." Her words caused a strange convulsion to grip his heart and a welcoming warmth to sweep through him. He smiled, watching as she stifled a yawn with the back of her hand.

"I think that's enough talk for tonight. Time for you to go to sleep." Nick stood up and headed for the doorway. "Good night, princess."

"Nick, wait!" She sat up in bed. "You forgot the most important thing of all."

"Your monster circle?" he asked, desperately trying to remember the magical words Violet had spoken the night before.

"No, I only need a monster circle when I have bad dreams." She smiled at him shyly. "You forgot to kiss me good-night."

Nick walked back over to her and kissed her soundly on the forehead, but before he could step back, she wrapped her arms tightly around his neck and gave him a sweet, feather-light kiss on his cheek. She smelled sweet and clean, and the feel of her small arms wrapped so tightly around him again made his heart flip-flop in his chest. "I love you, Nick," she whispered as she released him.

Murmuring a final good-night, Nick turned off her bedroom light and left the bedroom. Once outside her room, he expelled a deep breath. The kid was getting to him. She was definitely getting deep into his heart.

Thoughtfully he walked back down the stairs, pausing at the threshold of the living room, his gaze once again transfixed on the sleeping Violet.

It had been easy to dismiss their kiss the other night, easy to rationalize all the things that had made the kiss occur. It was much more difficult to dismiss the crazy tenderness he felt as he watched her sleeping.

He suddenly felt as if he'd been thrown into a pit of quicksand, and no matter how hard he fought, the end result was inevitable. Something was at work here, something strange and wonderful and more than a little bit frightening.

Violet and her daughter were affecting him in ways that nobody had ever affected him before. If he didn't know better, he would suspect Rachel's magical pixie dust of causing strange, disturbing thoughts in his head.

Yes, he had a feeling they were moving toward an inevitable end.... He just wasn't sure exactly what that end would be, and the uncertainty of it all scared the hell out of him.

Chapter Six

"Oh, Nick, I'm glad you're up," Violet greeted him as he came into the kitchen early the next morning. "I wanted to thank you for last night...putting Rachel to bed and everything." She rinsed her coffee cup and set it in the dish drainer. "I can't believe how I zonked out."

"That's why I got up early, so I'd have a chance to talk to you about the schedule you've been keeping." He moved over to the coffeepot and poured himself a cup of the fresh brew.

"I'm sorry. I just don't have time to talk this morning. I promised Mrs. Bodine I'd be over there early this morning." She grabbed her keys and purse off the kitchen table. "Rachel, it's time to go." She turned back to Nick. "And it's going to be another late night, so don't worry about holding dinner for us. We'll just grab a couple of hamburgers on the way home."

"Violet." As she began to walk by him, he grabbed her by the shoulders. He noticed that the dark smudges of exhaustion beneath her eyes had not disappeared overnight. If anything they had intensified, matching perfectly the pale purple blouse she wore. "Violet, I'm worried about you. You're driving yourself too hard."

Her face colored slightly and she moved away from his hands. "Nick, I really don't have time for this now." She checked her wristwatch and grimaced. "Rachel, let's go!" She smiled apologetically at Nick. "We'll talk tonight."

He nodded grudgingly.

Minutes later, as Violet drove to Mrs. Bodine's she thought of Nick's words. He was worried about her and the thought made a warm glow sweep through her. It had been a long time since anyone had worried about her. There were a lot of things about Nick that made her feel warm...like the memory of his kisses, the feel of his lips on her neck, his hands on her breasts.

She'd wanted to forget those few moments in the middle of the night, when desire had appeared out of nowhere and nearly consumed her. But the memory refused to be banished, refused to allow her a moment's peace.

She'd wanted him that night . . . wanted him still, and each moment spent with him, each conversation they had, no matter how mundane, the desire for him was there. It was a living, breathing entity between them.

But it was a desire she wouldn't—couldn't—follow through on. She was old-fashioned and she'd meant what she'd told him that night. She didn't want to make love unless she was in love, and she wanted her partner to feel the same way. And Nick didn't believe in love. A strange sadness lay heavy in her chest as she thought of his cynicism. How sad, not to believe in the special magic of love.

She parked her car in the Bodine driveway, shoving thoughts of Nick out of her mind. She was hoping to finish up this job in the next couple of days, which would give her a little over three weeks to finish the work on her own house.

Mrs. Bodine greeted her cheerfully. "I'm off to a meeting this morning," she said as Violet got busy. "I've been appointed to the refreshment committee for the town fair."

Violet smiled at the older woman. "You certainly keep busy. President of the Homes League, volunteer at the museum, secretary of the Ladies'

Auxiliary... and now the town fair. How do you ever find time for yourself?''

A small smile lifted the corners of Mrs. Bodine's thin lips. ''My dear, when you get to be my age and your husband has passed away and your children are grown with lives of their own, the last thing you want is time for yourself.'' She shrugged her impressive shoulders. ''When you're old and you find yourself alone, you learn to fill your life with causes and committees.'' Her smile turned self-conscious. ''Goodness, Mr. Bodine always did complain that I had a tendency to rattle nonsense in the mornings.'' She laughed. ''He always said my body got out of bed two hours before my brain.''

Her smile turned melancholy and she waved her hands impatiently. ''Goodness me, not even eight o'clock in the morning and here I am already getting maudlin.'' She watched for a moment as Violet cut a piece of wallpaper. ''I heard through the grapevine that you're entering your house in the Homes League contest.''

Violet nodded. ''I'm planning to if I can get the rest of my work completed.''

''My daughter Regina just loves your house. Every time we drive by it she comments on it. You've done wonders on the exterior.''

Violet smiled at the compliment. ''I just hope I can get the interior to reflect the same quality.''

"Oh, I'm sure you will," Mrs. Bodine assured her, looking around the room. "This is all coming along marvelously. You do wonderful work. Now, I must get out of here. I'll see you later this afternoon." With a wiggle of fingers, she grabbed her purse and left the house, leaving Violet alone to work in the silent big home.

As she worked, she thought of Mrs. Bodine. It seemed somehow sad that the old woman lived in this beautiful big home, yet ran to committee meetings and volunteer work, anything to keep her busy and out of the loneliness of the house.

There were some uncomfortable parallels between Mrs. Bodine's life and Violet's. Both had lost their husbands and both owned large Victorian homes.

However, I have Rachel to fill the void, Violet consoled herself. But she knew in her heart that there was no way a six-year-old girl could ever fill *all* the emptiness inside her.

There were some things only a man could give her, and she wasn't just concerned with the physical aspects. There were times when she hungered for the special smell of maleness, for a strong hand to reach out to hold hers. She longed for firmly muscled arms to hold her after a long day. She wanted the intimacy of sharing her thoughts, her dreams, her laughter with a special man.

Nick... Crazy that it was a vision of his face that instantly filled her mind. Her thoughts where he was concerned were all jumbled in her head, confused by the memory of his kiss, the feel of his body pressed against her.

She sat down on the floor, staring at the wallpaper waiting to be applied to the wall, her thoughts not on the paper, but rather on her boarder.

If she allowed herself, it would be very easy to fall in love with him. But of course that was something she couldn't allow.

She smiled ruefully and gave herself a mental kick in the behind. What was she doing wasting her time thinking about love and Nick? She had work to do. She didn't have time to indulge in ridiculous fantasies.

She worked until seven o'clock that evening, then packed up to leave, disappointed that she hadn't managed to complete the work. She'd have to come back the next day to finish up the trim.

"Mommy!" Rachel greeted Violet as she came through Doris's front door.

"Hi, sweetpea." Violet leaned down and gave her daughter a kiss, then straightened up and smiled tiredly at her mother. "Sorry I'm so late. I was hoping I could finish today, but I didn't."

Doris frowned. "You look terrible. You're working far too hard. You have plum-colored circles under your eyes."

"I'll rest up as soon as I finish Mrs. Bodine's place and the rest of the work on my house," Violet said.

"Why don't you sit down and let me fix you a cup of tea?" Doris urged.

Violet shook her head. "I'm exhausted. All I want to do is get home and relax." She turned and looked at Rachel. "Kiss Mimi goodbye."

"Mimi said I could go with her and Mr. Richardson to get ice cream," Rachel said, looking at her grandmother for confirmation.

"Indeed I did," Doris agreed. "I told her we'd ask you when you got here. I already fed her supper and we plan to walk downtown to get banana splits. We'll bring her back home later if it's all right with you."

Violet looked at her mother incredulously. "Mr. Richardson is going with you?" Doris nodded. "I can't believe he agreed to go," Violet said in surprise.

"Oh, he hasn't agreed. I haven't asked him yet. But I know he'll go." Doris's eyes twinkled brightly. "All that man really needs is for somebody to pay him some attention, and that's just what I'm going to do."

Suddenly Violet noticed that her mother had on makeup and that her hair was arranged in a different, more becoming fashion. She immediately realized that Doris was romantically interested in Mr. Richardson. The realization shocked her. Of all the men in Glenville, why on earth would her mother be interested in an old curmudgeon like Andrew Richardson? She smiled inwardly. Poor man, he didn't stand a chance against Doris's stubbornness and feminine wiles.

"So, can I go with them?" Rachel asked pleadingly.

Violet hesitated a moment then nodded. "Just make sure you try to have her home by bedtime," Violet told her mother, who nodded.

Minutes later, as she drove home, she thought about her mother and Mr. Richardson. Was it possible that beneath their constant bickering and insults was a spark of genuine affection? They both seemed to go out of their way to antagonize each other, and yet Violet now realized that after each confrontation with the old man her mother seemed more vibrant, more alive.

Violet smiled. Her mother had been alone for a long time. It would be nice to see her with a man in her life. Violet turned into her driveway, refusing to acknowledge the fact that she had the very same wish for herself.

It wasn't until she walked into the front door and smelled the savory scents that filled the air that she realized she hadn't eaten since breakfast.

"Ah, there you are," Nick exclaimed as she walked into the kitchen. "I was hoping you wouldn't be too much later, or the meat would have gotten dry." He removed the lid off the large pot on the stove and invited her to take a peek. "New England pot roast...your father's favorite recipe." He grinned. "I got it from your mother."

Violet looked at him blankly. "I told you I was going to be late tonight and that you didn't have to worry about holding supper." She noticed how at home he looked, relaxed in a pair of worn jeans and a short-sleeved light blue shirt. He looked as if he belonged right here, in her kitchen. She mentally shook herself, knowing these thoughts were dangerous ones.

Nick motioned for her to sit down at the table. "I didn't hold supper," he protested. "I planned it to be late to coincide with your schedule." He frowned suddenly. "Where's Rachel?"

Violet sank into a chair at the table. "She and my mother are taking Mr. Richardson out for ice cream." Nick raised a dark eyebrow in disbelief. "I know," Violet said with a small laugh, "it's crazy, but I think my mother has set her cap for Andrew."

Nick grinned. "That should be an interesting courtship." He placed the roast, potatoes and carrots onto a serving platter and set it on the table. He then grabbed a salad from the fridge and added it and a crusty loaf of bread to the spread.

"You're spoiling Rachel and me horribly," Violet said as he joined her at the table and they began to fill their plates. "How are we ever going to be able to go back to eating macaroni and cheese and cold oatmeal when you leave?"

He smiled, a soft one that creased the skin at the corner of his eyes and deepened their blue hue. "Maybe you need a little spoiling."

Violet flushed beneath the warmth of his gaze, looking down at the roast beef on her plate. "This all looks wonderful," she murmured, cutting into the tender piece of meat.

Nick watched her as she ate hungrily, enjoying the mere act of her satisfying her appetite. He could tell she was a sensual woman—it was there in the way she savored each bite, the way she closed her eyes and sighed as she bit into the crusty French bread.

He could imagine her closing her eyes that very same way as he tasted her lips, could envision the feel of her sigh against the side of his neck.

Since the night of Rachel's nightmare, the night he and Violet had allowed a flame of passion to burn out of control for too brief a time, he hadn't been able to stop thinking about that moment. No matter what he did during the day, his thoughts always returned to the feel of her body in his arms, the taste of her mouth against his.

He focused on the food on his plate. He wanted her. Big deal, he'd wanted other women in the past. Desire was nothing new, nothing alien. Rather it was an emotion he had dealt with before. Desire . . . his feelings for Violet were nothing more, nothing less than that.

As far as his concern for her, the strange sort of tenderness he felt toward her, that, too, was easily explained. He was a compassionate, caring sort of guy. He would feel the same way about anyone who'd had a rough time and was working herself half to death.

They ate in a companionable silence. Apparently Violet was too tired to indulge in idle conversation while she ate, and Nick was mentally formulating the conversation he intended to have with her before the night was over.

"So, what did you find to do to occupy your time all day today?" Violet asked as she shoved her plate aside and emitted a contented sigh.

"I trimmed the bushes on the north side of the house, ate lunch with Janet, then took a walk downtown." He grinned. "I met the Baskin sisters. This town seems to have more than its share of colorful characters."

Violet laughed. "The Baskin sisters are more colorful than most." The seventy-year-old triplets had never married, dressed exactly alike and wore their hair in the very same fashion. They lived together in a large house by the elementary school, where they often substitute taught.

"Have they always been so... identical? They even finish each other's sentences."

"Most of the people in Glenville believe they not only share the same physical traits, but the same brain, as well. I'll bet you met them in the park at around two o'clock."

He nodded. "They were there feeding the pigeons. How did you know?"

Violet smiled. "They're there every day at that time. And as far as Glenville having more than its share of colorful characters...that's not true. Every city and town have people who are slightly eccentric. Other towns maybe hide them better than we do." She paused thoughtfully, then continued. "In fact, I think everyone has certain habits and oddities of behavior."

"What about you?" he urged, an indulgent grin on his face. "What odd things do you do?"

Violet laughed. "Not fair. You brought up this conversation initially, so you have to go first."

Nick nodded agreeably. "I squeeze the middle of the toothpaste tube," he said after a moment of thought.

Violet shook her head. "Not good enough. Half the people in America do that." She grinned at him, feeling her exhaustion seeping away and a second wind filling her with a strange exuberance as she enjoyed the silliness of their conversation.

"I love popcorn and chocolate ice cream," he answered, looking at her expectantly.

Violet frowned. "That's not weird. I like popcorn and chocolate ice cream, too."

Nick grinned boyishly. "I like them mixed together."

She groaned. "That's not weird...that's gross!"

Nick laughed and she noticed what a warm shade of blue his eyes were, like the embracing waters of a sun-warmed swimming pool. "Your turn," he prompted.

She nodded, her brow creasing as she thought. "I like to sit up in the attic when it rains," she finally confessed.

"You mean up in my room?"

"No, above your room." She laughed at his look of disbelief. "I know, it's crazy. There's only a crawl space up there, and it's completely dark, but I love to sit up there and listen to the rain beating on the roof." She laughed again, this time self-consciously. "And now that we know each other's strangest oddities, we'd better get these dishes all cleaned up." She stood up and grabbed her plate.

"No, you don't," he protested, taking the plate out of her hand. "I'll clean up this mess. You go sit down and I'll make us coffee." When she sputtered a protest, he took her by the shoulders and guided her toward the living room. "You worked all day. I sat in the park and watched the Baskin triplets feed the pigeons. Now go."

Minutes later when he carried the coffee into the living room, Violet was ripping at the last of the wallpaper she'd been removing over the past couple of days. "Violet," he chided. "Can't you relax for a minute?" He sat down on the sofa and patted the space next to him. "Please come and sit down. I want to talk to you."

She did as he asked, her forehead wrinkled in curiosity.

He looked at her a moment, his gaze caressing her features. She was gorgeous. Even with the lines of fatigue, even with the dark circles beneath her eyes, she was the loveliest woman he'd ever seen. "I got up extra early this morning to talk to you—then you ran out of the house to work." He ran a hand through his hair in distraction, knowing he had no right to interfere in the way she lived her life, yet unable to stand by wordlessly and watch while she worked herself to death.

"What, Nick? What's so important?"

"First, before I forget—I promised a certain little inmate who's been confined to quarters for three days for throwing pixie dust that I'd speak to the parole board on her behalf."

Violet laughed and shook her head. "That little operator. What did she do? Make her bottom lip quiver? Cry alligator tears? Beg you to talk to me?"

"No, it was all my idea," Nick protested, then grinned. "Although she did manage to look pretty pitiful."

"Okay, I'll consider commuting her sentence," Violet agreed. "I just wish I knew what she was trying to accomplish by dousing you with red glitter."

Nick shrugged and reached up to touch his dark hair. "Maybe she's trying to magically make me a blonde like you two. But that's not the real reason I want to talk to you." His smile faded and he looked at her seriously. "I've been here for three weeks now—" He paused, surprised at how fast the past three weeks had gone by, dismayed to realize that meant he only had three weeks left here and then he'd fly back to his life in Chicago. "Anyway, for the past three weeks I've watched you knocking yourself out to please Mrs. Bodine. You get up before dawn, work all day on her place, then come home and work half the night here." He held up his hands to still whatever she was about to say. "I know, I have no right to interfere in your life. I'm just a boarder, but I can't stand seeing you so tired." He reached out and ran a finger lightly beneath one of her eyes. "I can't stand to see the dark circles here." He withdrew his touch and sighed. "I just don't understand why you're driving yourself to such lengths. Why must you work like a demon? Why don't you put off the work around here until you're finished at the Bodine place?"

"I can't," Violet answered. "If I'm going to enter the Homes League contest I have to have all these things around here completed within three weeks."

"The Homes League contest?"

She nodded, pausing a moment to pour them each a cup of coffee. "Each year the Homes League holds a contest for the house that's made the best renovations over the year. It was Bill's dream...our dream that we'd enter. Last year I couldn't. Bill had just died and there was just too much work to get done. I made a vow that nothing would stop me from entering this year." She paused, staring down into her coffee cup. When she looked back at him her eyes were a deep, vibrant purple of emotion. "I have to do it this year."

"It's so important to you?" he asked softly.

She nodded.

"What's left to be done?"

She pointed to the wall still needing to be stripped and wallpapered. "That wall. I need to finish the varnishing of the woodwork. I want to sand and varnish the entryway floor." She looked around the room critically. "And I guess that's about it."

"Let me help you," he urged.

"Oh, no, I couldn't let you do that," she protested.

"Please, I want to." He took her hands in his. "I have three weeks with nothing to do. If you don't put me to work I may find myself becoming a permanent fixture at the park with the Baskin sisters."

"Well . . ." She wavered.

"When will you be finished with the work at the Bodines'?"

"I should be able to finish up tomorrow."

"Great, then the following day you and I will work together to whip this place into shape."

Violet nodded, too touched by his offer to speak. She suddenly realized he still held her hands in his, the contact radiating a warmth through her. She knew she should get up, grab her coffee cup, do something to break the contact, but she couldn't.

She knew he was going to kiss her; she could see it in the way his eyes darkened to the color of midnight. And she wanted it, had been waiting to feel his lips against hers again. She leaned into him, wanting to let him know her want, her need. His eyes burned bright, the hot flame of blue fire and his lips descended toward hers.

"Yoohoo...we're home." The front door flew open and Doris's voice preceded them into the room. Nick and Violet sprang apart, Nick grabbing for his coffee cups as Violet jumped up to greet the threesome.

"Hello, how were the banana splits?" she asked, hoping her face wasn't as red as it felt.

"Terrible," Andrew answered gruffly. "They put on too much chocolate syrup and not enough whipped cream."

"Hmm...that didn't stop you from eating every bite of your own and half of mine," Doris protested.

"I liked mine," Rachel piped in.

"I'm glad." Violet smiled lovingly at her daughter. "Now, why don't you run upstairs and get into your pajamas? It's almost bedtime."

"Come on, old man. It's probably almost your bedtime, too," Doris said to Andrew, grabbing his arm possessively. "I want you nice and rested when I come to get you in the morning." She smiled at

Violet. "Andrew is going to help me clean out the basement tomorrow."

"It's a trade-off. I told her I'd help her tomorrow if she promises not to read my palm anymore," Andrew explained.

"But you didn't say anything about past-life regression," Doris reminded him.

"Past-life regression...bah...what nonsense," Andrew retorted, and as the two left, their voices rang out in strident tones until they reached Andrew's house.

"Uh...I'd better get upstairs and help Rachel," Violet said when she and Nick were once again alone. The moment for their kiss had passed and there was no way to recapture the mood. It was probably better this way, she thought. What was the point of sharing a kiss with a man who didn't believe in love and would be gone from her life in a matter of weeks? "Will you lock up?"

He nodded, smiling a good-night. When she had disappeared up the stairs, Nick leaned his head back on the sofa and closed his eyes. Talk about bad timing...Doris and Andrew got the prize. He'd wanted to kiss Violet so badly, and she'd wanted it, too.

He sighed, suddenly becoming aware of the sounds of Violet and Rachel completing their bedtime routine floating down the stairs. Soft mur-

murs, a childish giggle, the rustle of bedclothes being turned down... They were comforting sounds, ones that filled him with a strange sense of belonging.

Maybe it's something in the water, he thought, trying to come up with a logical reason for the insanity he felt all around him.

Andrew Richardson was suddenly becoming more human, subtly softening beneath Doris's attention. He himself sat here enjoying the noise of a woman tucking in a child, anticipating helping work on a house that wasn't even his. Yes, there was insanity in the air, and if he wasn't very careful, he was liable to get a fatal dose.

Chapter Seven

"Apprentice Elliot, reporting for duty."

Violet turned around from the stove and grinned at Nick, who was clad in a pair of paint-splattered overalls and a Cleveland Indians baseball cap. "Where did you get those?"

"Compliments of Joe." He swept the baseball cap off his head and sat down at the table. "I didn't pack any appropriate renovation clothes, so Joe kindly offered me the use of these." He sniffed the air appreciatively. "What smells so wonderful?"

Violet turned back around to face the stove. "I figured if I planned to work you half to death all day, the least I could do was start us off with a good breakfast."

"No cold oatmeal?"

She turned around just long enough to stick her tongue out at him. As she finished the breakfast preparations, Nick settled back in the chair, admiring the way the early-morning sunlight cascaded into the window and danced impishly in the strands of her pale hair. She looked rested this morning, and Nick knew it was because she'd gotten a full night's sleep.

She'd finished the Bodine job the day before and had come home thrilled because Mrs. Bodine had given her name to several of her friends. "Those friends of Mrs. Bodine's are always having rooms redone," she'd enthused to Nick over dinner the night before. "Hopefully, if my name gets around, and with Mrs. Bodine's influence, the jobs will be steady and Rachel and I won't have to worry."

As he watched her now, bustling around the kitchen, he hoped she was right. Happiness... prosperity... He wanted those things for her.

"Here we are, a hearty breakfast for a hard-working man." The plate she set before him held a huge omelet, hash brown potatoes and several pieces of golden brown toast.

Nick smiled at her appreciatively. "This looks wonderful." She blushed prettily and joined him at the table with a cup of coffee.

"Aren't you eating?" he asked with a frown.

"I already did. I ate with Rachel before I took her to Mom's."

While Nick ate, Violet sipped her coffee, studying him surreptitiously. He filled up her kitchen with his presence. As always, his very maleness enticed, teased her senses. His scent surrounded her, a male blend of shaving cream, spicy cologne and soap.

She closed her eyes for a moment, concentrating on memorizing his particular scent, knowing it was one of the many things she would miss when he was gone.

She opened her eyes and looked at him again, noting that his work outdoors had given his skin a rich, bronze tan. In the overalls without a shirt beneath, he looked more like a sexy women's magazine centerfold than a successful lawyer.

"Whatever made you decide to be a lawyer?" she asked, suddenly wanting to know everything there was to know about him.

He shrugged. "I've always loved the law. Initially I'd intended to be a lawyer specializing in contracts and big business. I worked with a large law firm for a couple of years doing just that, then decided to hang out my own shingle."

"So, how did you go from big business and contracts to being a divorce lawyer?"

"That was quite by accident." He paused a moment to finish his toast, then continued. "One of my friends was the son of a prominent, wealthy family. When he and his wife divorced, he asked if I'd represent him. I did and it turned out to be a high-profile, widely publicized case. When it was over I'd developed a reputation as the man to hire if you want a divorce."

"And do you like what you do?" she asked curiously.

He opened his mouth to answer, then closed it and frowned thoughtfully. He stared into his coffee cup, as if seeking the answer to her question there. "Six months ago I would have answered without hesitation that I loved my work. I found it challenging, stimulating, unpredictable. But lately... I don't know." He grinned at her. "I guess I need every day of my vacation to get over my case of burnout. Ask me again in another three weeks when I'm ready to go back home."

Back home... His words reverberated in Violet's head throughout the day as they worked together. The words were a constant reminder that he was only here for a brief time, then would be gone.

They worked most of the day on stripping off the old wallpaper of the remaining wall in the living room. It was a difficult task as there was a total of four layers of old paper to take off.

Nick proved to be a good worker. Although he'd never stripped paper before, he learned quickly what needed to be done and within minutes handled a scraper like a seasoned veteran.

He whistled while they worked, and soon Violet hummed along. It wasn't long before they were singing—old camp songs, favorite sing-alongs, beer-drinking classics. What Nick's voice lacked in tone, he compensated with volume, causing Violet's giggles to erupt frequently.

They had just finished a particularly rousing rendition of "Home on the Range" when Janet walked in, a pained expression on her face.

"What on earth are you two doing?"

"Working," Violet answered.

"And singing," Nick added.

"I certainly hope you're working better than you're singing," Janet observed, her blue eyes twinkling with warmth and humor.

Violet looked at her in mock outrage. "Are you insinuating that there's something wrong with our vocal skills?"

"Fie on you, woman," Nick explained to his sister. He grinned at Violet. "Poor Janet. She's always been tone-deaf."

"Ah, then that explains her lack of enthusiasm for our singing." Violet laughed as Janet looked at them both as if they'd lost their minds.

"I just stopped by to see if Violet and Rachel are available to come to a barbecue a week from this Saturday," Janet explained. "I know you'll be there," she added to Nick.

"Sure, what's the occasion?"

"Joe's fortieth birthday," Janet replied. "He doesn't want a big fuss, so we're inviting just a few people over to help us celebrate."

"Sounds like fun," Violet agreed.

"Well, this doesn't look like fun, so I think I'll get out of here before you put me to work like you did my poor brother." With a wiggle of her fingers, Janet disappeared out the door.

Violet and Nick worked until dinnertime, when Doris brought Rachel home. Doris refused their invitation to join them for supper, explaining that she and Andrew were eating dinner together.

"Looks like your mother's campaign to win Mr. Richardson is working," Nick observed as the three of them sat at the kitchen table eating dinner.

"Hmm... I guess love is in the air," Violet said, her gaze defying him to contradict her.

"Or loneliness," he countered with a challenging smile.

"Forever the cynic," Violet returned, shaking her head ruefully.

"What is a cynic?" Rachel asked curiously.

Violet smiled at her daughter. "That's somebody who doesn't believe in love or magic or pixies."

Rachel's eyes widened as she looked at Nick. "And you're one of those?" she asked.

"Well, maybe I believe a little bit in pixies," he answered.

"You'd better believe in them or they'll tie your shoelaces in knots and make you feel all sad inside," she cautioned.

"Well, I certainly don't want that to happen," he said with a laugh.

After dinner, Violet went back into the living room, intent on getting some more work done. She'd just picked up her wire brush and begun to climb the ladder when Nick and Rachel entered.

"Oh, no, you don't," he exclaimed, pulling her off the ladder and taking the wire brush out of her hand. "Eight hours of work a day is quite enough."

"But I just thought..."

"No way. You're not working anymore tonight," he said firmly. "Rachel and I had a powwow in the kitchen and we've decided it's a perfect night to watch movies and pop some popcorn."

Violet laughed and grinned at her daughter. "As far as Rachel is concerned, every night is a perfect night for movies and popcorn. Okay, okay." She relented as Nick and Rachel gave her their best puppy-dog looks. "How about you two pick out a movie and I'll go pop the corn."

"With lots of butter," Rachel requested eagerly.

Violet nodded and went back into the kitchen to make the treat. As she plugged in the electric popper and waited for the kernels of corn to burst, she could hear Nick and Rachel good-naturedly arguing over the choice of movies. The sound of his deep, rumbling voice followed by Rachel's high-pitched giggles, sent a wave of warmth sweeping through Violet.

This house had been lonely for laughter. She had been hungry for laughter, and like a starving man after a delicious feast, she felt sated . . . happy. The house seemed to settle, breathe a sigh of contentment around her.

She didn't want to think about how lonely and silent the house would be when he was gone. She refused to dwell on the unpleasant subject of his leaving. At this moment she was happy, and she didn't want any unwelcome thoughts to spoil the night.

When the popcorn was finished, she carried a large bowl into the living room, where Rachel and Nick were already seated on the sofa waiting for her. "Did you decide on a movie?"

"I wanted a crime drama and Rachel wanted a cartoon, so we decided to compromise," Nick explained.

Violet frowned. "I didn't realize there was a compromise between the two."

Nick held up a colorful video cover. "The Kung-fu Kats, crime fighters in a cartoon format."

"Ah, yes, of course." Violet laughed, joining them on the sofa as Nick punched the Play button of the remote control.

For the first hour of the movie, they all sat together on the sofa, enjoying the hot buttery popcorn and the silly antics of the cartoon characters on the screen. At some time during the middle of the movie, Rachel moved to the floor, stretching out on her tummy and propping herself up on her elbows to watch the picture. Within minutes, she'd melted down to the floor, sound asleep.

"Since the princess is sleeping, can we change this to a more adult movie?" Nick asked.

"And here I thought you were enjoying watching the Kung-fu Kats foil the evil intents of Dastardly Dog," Violet teased.

He grinned and clicked the tape off. "A little of this goes a long way." He got up off the sofa and checked her cache of recorded tapes. "Ah, now this is a movie," he exclaimed. *"Casablanca."* He put the videotape into the machine, then rejoined her on the sofa, sitting much closer than he had been before.

As the movie played, Violet had trouble focusing on it. She'd seen it a hundred times before and had always managed to lose herself in the bittersweet story, but this time all she could think about was Nick's closeness, the way his thigh pressed against hers, the warmth of his body so intimately near.

He moved his arm to rest on the back of the sofa behind her, then casually settled it onto her shoulders where his hand absently played with the ends of her hair.

At some point, she became aware of his gaze on her. Hot and hungry, his eyes lingered on her, as if willing her to turn and look at him. But she couldn't. She knew if she turned to him he would kiss her, and she wanted that more than anything...dreaded it more than anything.

All day long while they had worked together, laughed together, she'd been aware of the small flame of desire that had burned in his eyes, knew hers reflected the same hunger.

She knew exactly what was happening...knew that she was on the verge of falling head over heels in love with him. She couldn't turn and look at him. She refused to kiss him anymore. She had to maintain control of her heart.

"Uh, I should get her on up to bed," she said, jumping up off the sofa. "I'm really tired myself. I think I'll go on to bed, too."

"Don't you want to see the rest of the movie?"

She smiled tightly. "I've seen it hundreds of times. The end always makes me cry."

She knew she was running away from him, and she knew that he knew it. But there was something about the night, the intimacy of the moment and her own tumultuous emotions that frightened her. Leaning down, she picked Rachel up in her arms. "Good night," she told him, then hurried up the stairs, running from the desire in his eyes, wondering how far she'd have to run to escape the desire in her own heart.

Over the next week as they worked together on the house, Violet was careful not to stand too close to him, vigilant in not allowing any physical proximity of any kind, not wanting to give the passion between them an opportunity to flourish.

Nick seemed to feel the same way. They laughed together, were friendly, but he didn't cross the invisible barrier she'd erected to maintain the safety of her heart.

They fell into a comfortable routine, working together during the days, then spending the evenings doing fun things with Rachel. They played

miniature golf, went bowling and he taught them
both the fine art of eating chocolate ice cream and
popcorn mixed together.

The day before Janet and Joe's barbecue, Violet
awoke to the sound of rain peppering the house. It
was a soft rain that made a nice, comforting sound.
She smiled and snuggled deeper beneath the sheets.
Ah, the rain would be good on all the flowers Nick
had planted around the house. The breeze that
wafted in the partially opened window smelled
clean and sweet. She closed her eyes once again.

"Hey, lazybones, are you going to sleep all
day?"

She awoke abruptly to the sound of Nick's voice
and a loud rap on her bedroom door. She rolled
over and looked at her clock radio, horror sweeping over her as she saw the time. Nine o'clock. Oh
God, Rachel was late for school.

She jumped out of bed and ran to the door,
throwing it open and colliding with Nick who stood
on the other side. "Whoa." He laughed, grabbing
her by the shoulders.

"Rachel...she'll be late for school," she gasped
frantically.

"She's already gone. We had breakfast together
and then I drove her to school. Hope you don't
mind that I borrowed your car."

"Uh, no... Thanks for taking care of her...."

"No problem," he returned, not taking his hands off her shoulders. God, she was beautiful with her hair tousled around her head like a gleaming halo and her eyes the deep violet of dusk's light. The pale blue nightgown hugged the curves of her body, allowing him a glimpse of the rounded tops of her breasts.

He wanted her so badly, it was an ache inside him that wouldn't go away. Working next to her the past week, smelling her scent, watching her laugh, had been an exquisite form of torture. He didn't realize he was caressing her shoulders until she stepped away from his touch.

"I'll just go get dressed, and we can get to work," she murmured, disappearing back into her bedroom and closing the door behind her.

Nick stood for a moment in the hallway staring at her door. He didn't want to work. What he wanted to do was enter her bedroom, lift her up in his arms and take her to bed. He wanted to make love to her while the gentle rain beat its rhythm against the windows. He wanted to explore her mysteries, her warmth as they lay naked together beneath the sheets.

But he knew he couldn't. She wanted love, and that wasn't what he had to offer her. With a heavy sigh, he went back downstairs to the kitchen.

By the time he'd made a fresh pot of coffee, she joined him. Clad in a pair of jeans and a pink T-shirt, she looked as fresh as a newly budded flower.

"Mmm, thanks," she said as he poured her a cup of the coffee and placed it before her on the table.

She sipped it gratefully, then smiled. "I can't believe I overslept. Thank you for getting Rachel off to school."

"No problem. We made a deal. She promised not to hit me with the glitter this morning and I promised to make her pancakes for breakfast."

"I didn't realize she was still getting you with her glitter," Violet said.

"Now don't yell at her," Nick said hurriedly. He grinned. "She only gets me when I least expect it."

"The pixie dust was my mother's idea," Violet explained.

"Now why doesn't that surprise me?" He laughed.

Violet grinned wryly. "Anyway, Rachel had some adjustment problems when she first came to live with Bill and me. The pixie dust seemed to help." The telephone jangled shrilly, interrupting the conversation. With a smile of apology, she got up to answer.

As she spoke on the phone, Nick drifted into the living room to look at the work they had left to do. They'd finished stripping and varnishing the woodwork and it gleamed in natural beauty. The walls were nearly ready for the paper she'd bought, a pale blue-and-peach-floral print. Another couple of days and the work would be completed. She could then enter the contest that seemed so important to her. He felt a wonderful sense of satisfaction that he'd been a part of helping her achieve her goal.

"Nick!"

He turned as she flew in the room, her face wreathed in a radiant smile. "That was Mrs. Craigmont, a friend of Mrs. Bodine's. She wants me to wallpaper her bedrooms...seven of them!" She laughed in abandonment and threw herself in his arms. "Oh, Nick, don't you know what this means? Perhaps I'll earn enough extra money to buy a new furnace."

"That's terrific," he said huskily, her body warmth as welcomed as a blanket on a frigid night. He grinned at her. "You're the only woman I know who when she earns a little extra money gets excited about buying a furnace."

She moved out of his arms self-consciously. "Someday I'll be able to afford to buy all the wants—right now I have to keep focused on our needs. And sooner or later winter will come and we'll need a new furnace."

"When do you start the new job?" he asked, wishing she was still in his arms, feeling strangely bereft without her there.

"Next Monday, so I'd better get to work here, finish up what I can this weekend."

"Before we get started, there's one thing I insist we do." He took her hand in his and started up the stairs.

"What?" she asked as he pulled her along. "Nick, what are you doing?"

He smiled back at her mysteriously as he led her up to his room on the third floor. "I've shared my popcorn and ice cream secret eccentricity with you, even taught you the proper way of eating it. Now it's raining and I think it's only fair that you show me this oddity you have of spending rainy days up in the attic."

Her smile lit up her face. She walked over to the corner of the room and yanked on a rope that hung from a trapdoor in the ceiling. A set of wooden stairs descended and she motioned for him to follow her up.

As he climbed behind her, he noted again the enticing wiggle of her bottom, the sweet scent that emanated from her. "Be careful. You have to crawl so you won't bump your head."

As they crawled away from the opening, it became so dark Nick could only see the faint outline of her body as he followed her.

This is ridiculous, he thought as he swatted away a cobweb that tried to swallow his head. What on earth am I doing crawling around in a dusty old attic? There were dust bunnies up here the size of lions. He'd lost his mind—that was the only explanation.

"Rachel and I always sit right here," she said, waiting a moment as he seated himself beside her. "You can get the best effect here."

"I've decided your eccentricity is definitely stranger than mine," he grumbled, feeling like more than half a fool.

She laughed and took his hand in hers. "The first time I brought Rachel up here, she thought I was half-crazy, too. But give it a minute. Lean your head back and listen. Rachel believes that the sound of the rain on the roof is really pixies with tap shoes dancing in merriment."

Nick merely grunted and leaned his head back, wondering what on earth had possessed him to indulge her in this nonsense.

The darkness was complete around them, like a mother's womb enfolding them securely. After a moment or two Violet leaned her head against his shoulder, her hand still clasping his.

He could smell her, the provocative, fresh scent he would always identify as hers alone. He placed an arm around her, pulling her head back against his shoulder. With the tips of his fingers he lightly caressed the softness of her cheek. She breathed into his neck, a sweet release of contentment.

Nick closed his eyes, at peace with the moment, happy with her in his arms. And instantly he realized the possibility of magic . . . for as he listened to the rain, it did, indeed sound like pixies tap-dancing across the roof.

Chapter Eight

"Ah, the room is looking great," Doris enthused, walking around the living room and eyeing the newly papered walls.

"Only one wall left and the room is done," Violet said with satisfaction.

"You've done a wonderful job."

Violet smiled. "I couldn't have finished it all so quickly without Nick's help."

"Ah, yes, where is the handsome barrister this fine morning?" Doris asked as the two women moved into the kitchen.

"He and Rachel are already over at Janet's. They went early to help her and the boys decorate the backyard for Joe's birthday barbecue." Violet poured them each a glass of ice tea, then joined her mother at the table.

"Rachel sure has taken to Nick. It will be hard on her when he leaves," Doris observed. "How much longer will he be here?"

"Two weeks," Violet answered, hoping the hollowness in her stomach wasn't evident in her tone of voice. "How are you and Andrew getting along?" she asked, quickly changing the subject, not wanting to think about Nick returning to Chicago.

"Fine. Everything is just fine." Doris frowned.

"Mother, is something wrong?" Violet asked. Her mother had seemed rather preoccupied since she'd walked in. Violet looked at her curiously.

"Not wrong, really. But something is rather strange." She looked at Violet, her bright blue eyes emitting bewilderment. "I've lost Paul."

Violet stared at her mother blankly. How did one go about losing a ghost who lived in the attic? "What do you mean, you've lost him?"

"He's gone. Even his vibrations are gone from the attic. It's as if he was never there." Doris shook her head and sighed. "It's all so very strange. One day he was there, and the next day he was gone. I think it's Andrew. Paul left when Andrew started coming over." A frown furrowed her brow. "I think Andrew must have frightened him away."

Violet had another thought on the matter. The ghost had appeared in the attic at a time when her mother had been desperately lonely. Now that Doris had Andrew, Violet suspected her mother didn't need Paul anymore. But she saw the confusion and worry on her mother's face and she covered the older woman's hands with hers. "Mother, maybe Paul finally discovered the way to get out of the spirit world and back into circulation. Perhaps he's found somebody to make a new life with."

Doris's face brightened. "Oh, I certainly hope so. I so want him to be happy."

"And you're happy?"

Doris nodded, a faint blush on her face. "That old curmudgeon makes my heart flutter like it hasn't done for years." She laughed self-consciously. "Silly, isn't it. At my age—to feel like a teenager again."

"It isn't silly at all. I think it's wonderful." Violet squeezed her mother's hands, then released them. "Are you and Andrew going to the barbecue?"

"We wouldn't miss it. Andrew is bringing his special spareribs and I baked two pies." She looked at her watch. "In fact, I probably should get home and change clothes. I've got to pick Andrew up in an hour." She stood up and smiled at Violet. "We'll see you in a little while."

Violet remained at the table after her mom had left, sipping her ice tea thoughtfully. Two weeks. The thought filled her both with dread and relief.

If she could just maintain control of her emotions for another two weeks then he would be gone, out of her life. There would be an empty space, a silence in her heart, but eventually it would go away and she would heal.

The next boarder who rented her room would be older than sixty or a woman. She never again wanted a man beneath her roof who was young, attractive and virile. But she had a feeling no other man, no matter what he looked like, would ever affect her like Nick had. Nick was special, and in two weeks he would be gone.

She released a sigh of disgust and stood up, deciding if she hurried she could get up another strip of wallpaper before she had to change clothes and head over to Janet's.

"Happy birthday, Joe," Violet greeted her neighbor as she walked in their front door, kissing him soundly on the cheek.

"Thanks, Violet." He hugged her, then gestured toward the sliding doors. "Everyone else is out in the backyard."

"You're the guest of honor—why aren't you out there?"

Joe gestured to the baseball and bat on the sofa. "I just came in to get those. Your mother, Nick and Rachel have challenged me and my boys to a little game of ball."

"This I've got to see," Violet said with a laugh, heading for the sliding doors. She stepped out into the bright sunshine, grateful that the rain from the day before hadn't been enough to ruin the outdoor event.

"Mommy, Mommy, I've got a balloon!" Rachel ran over to greet Violet, in her hand she clutched a bright red balloon.

"Somebody had a lot of hot air," Violet said. Balloons were everywhere, tied to crepe paper, floating on the ground, hanging from the trees.

"Me," Nick answered, joining Violet and Rachel. "And no more wisecracks about hot air."

"Wisecracks?" Violet smiled at him innocently. "I was just commenting on how nice all the decorations look."

"Rachel and I make a great team when it comes to blowing up balloons and hanging crepe paper, don't we, princess?"

Rachel nodded, grinning up at Nick.

"And now we're going to see what kind of a baseball team we make, right?"

"Right!" Rachel agreed, laughing as Nick tweaked her nose.

"Come on, Nick, Rachel...Doris...!" Joe yelled from the center of the yard. "Let's play ball!"

Violet smiled indulgently as Nick and Rachel ran toward where Joe and his three boys stood waiting for them. She waved to her mother as the older woman ran toward the group of players.

"Damn fool woman. Hope she doesn't get hurt," Andrew said, coming to stand beside Violet. "I told her she was too old for such nonsense, but she doesn't listen to me."

Violet smiled sympathetically. "You should know by now that Mother doesn't think she's too old for anything."

Andrew nodded, his gaze on Doris, who stood at home base swinging a bat. "You know I'll probably marry her."

Violet looked at the old man, surprised to see his face color in a blush. "Oh?"

"Well, somebody needs to take care of her," he said as if in defense. "She doesn't have half a lick of sense."

Violet placed her hand on Andrew's arm. "She could use a man like you," she agreed. "She needs somebody strong and good, somebody who can appreciate her."

Andrew nodded, then grunted. "Guess I'll go over and check the ribs. Nobody ever grills them quite right."

Violet smiled as she watched him go over to the grill, where he apparently instructed Janet on the fine art of barbecuing ribs. She grinned widely as Janet handed Andrew the fork and left him in charge.

"Why is it that all men think they know how best to cook outside?" Janet asked as she approached Violet.

Violet laughed. "I guess it has something to do with the fresh air and the scent of meat cooking over an open flame. It throws them back to Neanderthal thinking."

Janet laughed, motioning for Violet to join her in one of the lawn chairs. "Ah, thank goodness it's a nice day. I had nightmares last night about it pouring down rain and ruining everything." She grinned at Violet. "Hey, I heard you got another job. Congratulations."

"Thanks, I start Monday. I'm hoping I can finish up my living room tomorrow so I won't have to keep up the crazy pace of the last month."

"Nick said you've been working yourself half to death."

Violet shrugged. "It takes a lot of work to keep up that house."

Janet frowned. "You know, as much as I hate to say it—I'd be unhappy if you moved—but if you were smart you'd sell that house and move into something more manageable.''

"You know I can't do that," Violet protested, then admitted softly, "although I have to admit there are times I think that doesn't sound like such a bad idea."

Janet nodded, and for a moment the two of them fell silent. "Looks like they're having fun," she said, referring to the baseball game taking place in the center of the yard.

Violet nodded, her gaze captured by Nick. He stood in center field, waiting to capture any of Doris's pitches that might be successfully hit. The sunshine played in the dark richness of his hair, pulling out hints of warm red hues. Clad in a pair of cutoff jean shorts and a T-shirt, he looked gorgeous.

She smiled, watching as Nick encouraged Rachel, who stood at first base. Despite his protests about love and marriage, Violet realized he'd make a wonderful father. He had a natural ease with the kids, an insurmountable amount of patience and a genuine humor that drew children to him.

"You're in love with him."

"I beg your pardon?" She flushed and looked at Janet quizzically.

Janet smiled knowingly. "Nick. You are in love with him."

Violet started to protest, wanting to scream that it wasn't true, couldn't be true. But it was. She looked down at her hands, for a moment unable to answer, then she slowly shook her head. "Yes, I am," she answered softly, her voice reflecting her misery. "For all the good it does me." She folded her hands in her lap, staring down at them. "I'm in love with him and he's going back to his life in Chicago in two weeks."

"I wouldn't be so sure about that," Janet said, causing Violet to look at her curiously.

"What . . . what do you mean?"

Janet shrugged. "Just that Nick was asking Joe questions the other night about maybe moving his law practice here. I think Nick's tired of the big city. He likes Glenville."

Hope buoyed up inside of Violet, causing a rush of emotions to rise in her throat. He might stay, her heart sang joyously. He might stay.

The hope was short-lived as she realized it didn't matter. Even if he decided to move his practice here, make Glenville his home. It didn't change the fact that Nick didn't believe in love, and Violet didn't believe in doing without love. Whether Nick decided to live in Glenville or not, any relationship between the two of them was hopeless . . . utterly hopeless.

* * *

Rachel's scream awakened Violet, who instantly realized the little girl was suffering another nightmare. She stumbled from her bed and headed across the hall, pausing at the doorway as she realized Nick had beat her to it and was already there, soothing the little girl. Violet remained in the hallway, watching the two of them.

"Hey, princess," he crooned, taking Rachel into his arms. "It's all right. I'm here."

Rachel clung to him, her shoulders shaking with convulsive sobs. "Help me, I'm scared."

"It's all right. I won't let anything happen to you," Nick said softly, stroking her hair gently. "I won't let anything hurt you. It was just a bad dream . . . a nightmare. It's over now."

He took her face in his hands, smiling down at her and wiping away the tears that streaked down her face. "Besides, you're the pixie princess, and nothing can hurt you."

Rachel sniffed audibly. "But . . . but sometimes I'm not the pixie princess," she explained tearfully. "Sometimes I'm just a scared little girl."

Nick laughed and kissed the end of her nose. "Remember when you felt my muscles and you said they were as big as Popeye?"

Rachel nodded, her blue eyes huge as she gazed at him.

"Don't you think Popeye could fight off any monsters that bothered him?"

She thought about it for a moment, then nodded. "I guess."

"If my muscles are as big as Popeye's, then I should be able to fight off any monsters who bother you."

A dubious expression crossed Rachel's features. "Maybe I should feel your muscle again."

Nick nodded and flexed his arm. Rachel ran her hand over his muscle and smiled in satisfaction. "And you'd fight any monster who came to get me?" she asked.

"I'd twist them in knots and eat them like pretzels," Nick exclaimed.

Rachel giggled, then yawned widely, her eyelids at half-mast. Nick tucked her back in beneath the blankets and placed a tender kiss on her forehead. "You keep the monsters away," Rachel said, more than half-asleep.

"I will." He brushed a strand of her hair off her forehead.

"Draw the monster circle," she whispered.

Violet smiled, watching as he got up and pointed his finger. He didn't get the words quite right, and Violet winced and stifled a giggle as he banged his shin on the edge of the bed. But it seemed to satisfy Rachel.

"Stay here until I go back to sleep," she said when he was finished with the magical chant.

He sat back down on the edge of the bed. "I won't go anywhere until you're in happy dreamland."

"I love you, Daddy," she murmured, more asleep than awake.

There was a moment of hesitation, then Nick answered softly. "I love you, too, princess."

Violet's heart slammed against her rib cage. She leaned against the hallway wall, not wanting Nick to know she'd witnessed the scene with Rachel.

She needed to think...assess. Nick protesting that he didn't believe in love suddenly seemed like the empty words of a frightened man. He loved Rachel. It was evident in his words, his gentle ways.

And what does he feel for me? she wondered. She knew he wanted her, desired her, but now she realized that perhaps his feelings for her transcended a mere physical longing. He cared about her, he worried about her. What else but love could make a man crawl up into an attic on a rainy day? What else but love would make a man get up in the middle of the night to soothe a little girl's fears?

She looked at him as he came out of the bedroom. He smiled as he saw her. "She had a nightmare. She's back asleep now."

She nodded, uncertain how to act with all that whirled around in her head. "Uh...thanks," she murmured.

"How about some tea? It's what the doctor orders following intense nightmares." He smiled and she nodded.

Together they walked down the stairs and into the kitchen where he placed the teakettle of water on to boil.

Violet leaned with her back against the counter, still not knowing what to say, wondering if there was any hope for anything real, anything lasting between them.

"The barbecue was fun today, wasn't it," he said, apparently not noticing anything amiss in her silence. "Joe sure had a good time." He chuckled. "And we gave them a tromping in the baseball game. Rachel is quite a first baseman."

She nodded, her gaze lingering hungrily on his bare back as he grabbed the cups and tea bags from the cabinet. God, how she loved him. If he left Glenville in two weeks as he was supposed to, there was no way she would be left unscarred. Somehow, someway, her love had become too intense, he was buried too deeply in her heart not to leave a gaping wound when he left.

She had to know how he felt about her. She needed to know if she should foster hope, or if she should prepare herself for a heartbreak of monumental proportions.

The teakettle hissed and he moved it off the burner, then turned and looked at her, as if aware for the first time of her unnatural silence.

"Are you all right?" he asked, his brow wrinkled in concern.

She shook her head and approached him. "Nick..." As she breathed his name, she placed her hand on his bare chest and that was all it took for him to answer her nonverbal plea.

With a deep, guttural groan, he gathered her into his arms and covered her mouth with his. His lips were hot, hungry, demanding the response she eagerly gave. She opened her mouth to him, wanting him to kiss her so deeply, she would never recover.

As he kissed her, moaning her name into her mouth, she knew there was more than passion, there was more than desire. His love was in the kiss, whether he knew it or not. She felt it there, she tasted its sweetness.

She gasped breathlessly, as in one smooth movement he lifted her up to straddle his waist, her nightgown riding up past her thighs as her legs locked around him. His lips slid down her neck, nipping and licking, teasing her into a frenzy. She clung to him, molding her body against his as his mouth once again claimed hers in a fiery kiss that stoked the fires of her insides.

He walked over to the table and gently sat her on the edge, at the same time lifting up her nightgown and removing it over her head. He threw it to the floor, where it landed, a pool of forgotten blue silk.

Despite the brightness of the kitchen light, clad only in a pair of wispy panties, Violet felt no embarrassment, no shame. As his hands covered her breasts she saw the stark desire that radiated from his eyes. She felt the physical proof of his arousal as he leaned into her, and she was lost.

He kissed her breasts softly, causing her nipples to surge and tighten in eagerness. His hands moved down to stroke the sensitive inner flesh of her thighs. She tangled her hands in his hair, wanting him closer...closer. She arched against him, wanting him to take her, possess her, mark her forever as his alone.

He moaned her name and raised his head to look at her. His eyes were midnight blue pools containing an unspoken question.

"Yes," she answered him. "Please, Nick, make love to me."

His eyes flamed at her words and he pulled her up and into him, tangling his hands in her hair, kissing her throat in wild abandon.

Violet closed her eyes, on fire with her need, inflamed by her love. "Yes," she whispered. "Oh, Nick, I love you so." The words escaped her unconsciously, but she instantly knew they were a mistake.

He stiffened against her, then moved away from her. He ran a hand through his hair in almost angry distraction. When he looked at her again, his eyes were no longer a warm blue, but rather a dismal black. "Dammit, Violet. Why did you have to say that?" he demanded.

And in that instant, the hope that had been in her heart deflated, leaving behind only a dull, aching emptiness.

Chapter Nine

Violet suddenly felt naked...cold and vulnerable. The light overhead was harsh and glaring. She slid off the table and reached for her nightgown, her hands trembling as she drew the blue silk garment over her head.

She was aware of Nick's gaze on her, dark with anger, bleak with frustration. He backed against the countertop, staring at her as if she'd suddenly developed a dread disease. "Why did you have to say that?" he repeated, his voice terse and sharp.

"I only said what I feel in my heart," she answered softly. She looked at him, her love aching inside of her. "Nick..." She reached out and lightly touched his shoulder. "What are you so afraid of?"

He jerked away from her touch as if her fingers held a hornet's sting. His body was rigid, his muscles taut. His face was twisted in angry torment. "I'm not afraid of anything," he retorted. "I told you from the very beginning that I didn't believe in love. The whole concept is nothing but a myth, a ridiculous fantasy." He laughed, an ugly sound filled with scorn. "I've gotten quite wealthy because people continue to fall for the myth of love and marriage and happily ever after. It's all just a head game."

"But that's not true," Violet protested. She clenched her hands into fists at her side, trying to control the overwhelming need to touch him, to connect with him, to somehow make him believe in the magic. "What about all the people who remain happily married for years and years?" she asked softly.

"Like my parents?" He laughed again, the same ugly sound. "They were together for twenty-two years, then decided it had all been a mistake." His dark eyebrows rose cynically.

"Is that what this is all about? The divorce of your parents made you believe that love didn't exist?"

"That was merely my first introduction into the reality of love."

"What about Janet and Joe, who are building something real and lasting between them, whose love for each other is open and visible for everyone to see?"

"They're the exceptions, not the rule. I told you, Violet. I see the aftermath of marriage, when the sacred vows crumble and somebody walks away. I've seen the hatred that replaces love, the bitterness that fills hearts. I don't want any part of it. Nobody will ever walk away from me." His voice rang with conviction.

Violet felt him slipping away from her and she filled with an empty, deep despair. "Nick, you can't tell me that you don't feel something for me. It's been building and growing between us for the past month."

He released a deep sigh, running his hand once again through his hair. He gazed at her for a long moment, not saying anything, his eyes losing some of their blackened intensity. "No, I can't deny that there is something special between us. I care about you, I care what happens to you. I enjoy being with you, and I want you."

"It's more than that," Violet whispered, her voice trembling with her emotions. "Lots of people find a special magic that keeps them loving each other for a lifetime. We have that magic, Nick."

She took his hand and placed it against her chest. "I know it. I feel it here, in my heart."

"You and your magic," he scoffed, yanking his hand away, stepping back to physically distance himself from her. "What you need is a good stiff dose of reality, and the reality is that you have a kid who's been allowed to indulge herself in fantasy. She carries pixie dust and believes in monsters. You have a mother who has the ghost of Paul Revere living in her attic." He paced the length of the kitchen, his voice raised in frustration. The words shot out of him rapidly, like a machine gun spitting a volley of bullets. "Reality is, you're working yourself to death on this house, trying to fulfill a dream that's not even yours, but your dead husband's. This house is nothing but a money pit, eating up your finances and sucking the very life out of you. No magic, Violet. Just reality. Reality, Violet, face reality."

Violet stared at him, shocked at his words, angered by his nerve. "How dare you . . ." The words escaped her on a hiss of rage. "How dare you presume to tell me to face reality." Her anger bubbled out of her like champagne from a shaken bottle, explosive and unexpected, it spewed. "Let me tell you something. Bill and I adopted Rachel when she was two years old. Her parents were alcohol-and-drug abusers who physically neglected and abused her. They finally abandoned her in a rat-infested apartment. She was there alone for three days and nights before somebody finally heard her crying. A baby left alone for three days and nights..." Violet swiped at her cheeks, surprised to discover tears. She trembled with her rage as she eyed him. "If she needs protective monster circles drawn around her bed and a bag of glitter to finally feel safe and secure, then so be it. She's had enough reality to last a lifetime."

Nick's face visibly paled. "I'm sorry... I had no idea."

"No, you didn't," Violet returned, the anger seeping out of her on a whoosh of air. She looked at him sadly. "There's a lot you don't know. We all have our personal demons, Nick. Demons we deal with as best we can. Maybe it's time you faced your own." With a choking sob, she turned and ran from the room.

Nick started to go after her, but stopped himself. If he did go after her, what would be accomplished? Nothing would be changed. The end result would be the same.

He sat down at the kitchen table and released a shuddery sigh. How had everything gotten so screwed up? When had everything become so complicated? Things would have been fine if she hadn't told him she loved him. It had all been great, it had

all been wonderful...until she'd breathed those
words so softly against his neck.

He slammed his fist down on the tabletop. Why
in the hell had she ruined it all, complicated things?
He covered his face with his hands.

It had been bad enough when Rachel had whispered, "I love you, Daddy." For a moment when
he'd heard those words, he'd thought his heart had
stopped in his chest. But he'd been able to dismiss
those words as the sleeping, confused mutterings of
a six-year-old. Violet's words were much more difficult to dismiss.

For the past week, as the end of his vacation had
grown nearer, dread had clutched him as he thought
of going back to his life in Chicago.

He liked Glenville. He'd played around with the
idea of moving his law practice here. He'd begun to
think that he could build a life here, enjoy the kind
of life-style the small town offered. But that was
before Violet had breathed those dreaded words to
him. Love... He wanted no part of it. He needed
no part of it.

He suddenly had an urgent desire to escape
Glenville, run from Violet and the little pixie princess and get back to his real life in Chicago.

Violet awoke, feeling as if it had only been minutes before when she'd finally drifted off to sleep.

Her eyes felt gritty and she knew it was a result of the residue of tears and too little sleep. She looked at her clock radio. It was only a little after seven and she knew she'd been awake almost all night.

She rolled over on her back, staring at the ceiling as she played and replayed the scene with Nick. It all seemed like a bad dream . . . a nightmare. If only he would realize what they had, if only he'd open his heart to the possibility of love. If only. . . Her eyes misted, causing the tiny cracks in the ceiling to blur and blend together. With a sigh she closed her eyes.

She was humiliated, angry and somehow saddened by Nick's vehement denial of the existence of love. It made a mockery of all she'd felt for him, everything they had shared.

"You're a fool, Violet Sanders," she said aloud, knowing the fault for this whole mess was not entirely Nick's. She had to take some responsibility, as well.

It was true, he had been honest and open with his cynicism. He'd warned her that his heart wasn't looking for a commitment. She'd listened with her ears, but her heart apparently hadn't heard his words. And if it had heard, her heart had refused to believe.

He would be here for two more weeks. How would she ever survive seeing him for fourteen more days, seeing him every day and knowing there would never be anything between them? How could she get through the days, smelling his evocative scent, hearing his rich, warm laughter...how could she live with him...love him for fourteen more long days?

Reluctantly, she sat up, knowing that hiding in her room for the next two weeks was not an option. She had to face him sooner or later, and it might as well be first thing this morning.

She got out of bed and dressed quickly in a pair of denim shorts and a purple, short-sleeved blouse. If she hurried, she could probably get the last couple strips of wallpaper up before Rachel awoke and demanded her breakfast.

Once in the kitchen she breathed a sigh of relief, hearing no noise from the upstairs quarters, realizing that the morning-after confrontation wouldn't take place immediately.

She poured the water through the coffee machine, then leaned against the counter waiting for it to drip through. As she stood there, her gaze unconsciously went to the table, where she had sat the night before and enjoyed the splendor of being in Nick's arms.

She fought against the memories that assaulted her mind, the feel of his thick hair tangling around her fingers, the hot, hungry caress of his lips against her skin. How could she forget the splendor of his hands caressing her breasts, the wonder of her heart quickening with each of his kisses?

She closed her eyes, needing to forget, but knowing that some small part of her wanted to retain the memories forever, keep them locked inside to be brought out on cold, lonely nights. Even now, her body responded to the visions her mind provided, causing her knees to weaken, her heart to flutter, a warmth to invade the pit of her stomach.

She sensed more than heard somebody in the room with her. She opened her eyes and saw him standing in the doorway of the kitchen. Clad in a business suit, white shirt and tie, he looked more than ever like a successful lawyer. But more than his attire, it was the distance in his eyes that cut her like a knife, twisted her heart into a mangled mess. Her eyes widened as she noticed his suitcase sitting on the floor beside him.

"Uh...I'm flying back to Chicago this morning," he said awkwardly, his gaze not quite meeting hers. "I've already called for a cab. It should be here anytime."

"Oh...you're cutting your vacation short." She was surprised at how normal, how natural her voice sounded, not reflecting the turbulent emotions that raged inside her.

"Yeah, well, things have probably been piling up back at the office. I figured it was time I got back to work—"

"I understand," Violet interrupted him, not wanting to hear any excuses, any vague reasons for his sudden departure. They both knew why he was going. He was running away, and nothing she said or did would stop his flight.

A car horn sounded from outside.

"That must be my cab," he said, his eyes making contact with hers for the first time. She tried to read the expression there, but it was inscrutable, the muddled blue of storm-laden skies. "Thanks for everything," he offered awkwardly.

"No problem," she answered tersely. *Anytime you want to steal a heart while on vacation, think of me.*

They both turned as Rachel came stumbling down the stairs, rubbing her eyes, her hair sleep-tousled around her head. "Hi," she said, smiling sleepily at first Violet, then Nick. "What are you guys doing?" Eyeing Nick's suitcase, she frowned. "Are you going somewhere?"

Nick grimaced painfully and bent down on one knee so he was eye level with the little girl. Rachel immediately sidled up next to him and placed an arm around his neck, gazing trustingly at him. "It's time for me to go home, Rachel," he explained.

"You knew I was just staying upstairs during my vacation. Now it's time for me to go back to my real home in Chicago."

She stared at him for a long moment. Her lower lip quivered ominously and she tightened her grip around his neck. "But I don't want you to go back to Cago."

"I know. I'm sorry, but I have to." Nick stood up, smiling brightly at Rachel. "But I'll write to you. We can be pen pals." His smile faltered as Rachel turned and ran back up the stairs. A second later her bedroom door slammed shut.

He turned and looked at Violet, his features twisted with regret. "I'm sorry."

"Don't worry. She'll be fine." Violet's heart jumped spasmodically in her chest and suppressed tears prickled beneath her eyelids. "You'd better not keep your taxi waiting."

He nodded and picked up his suitcase. He walked to the front door, Violet following behind. He started out, then turned back and looked at her. "Violet . . . I'm sorry that—"

"Just go," she exclaimed tensely, unsure how long she could maintain her control. She grabbed tightly to the wood of the door, almost welcoming the pain of the roughness against her fingertips. "Please, just go," she whispered in torment.

He hesitated a moment longer, then turned and
walked toward the cab. He was just about to climb
into the backseat when she stepped out of the door
and called his name. He turned and looked at her
hesitantly.

"Just remember, Nick, you're the one walking
away." She didn't wait for his answer. She closed
the door and leaned against it, the tears she'd tried
so hard to control seeping out from beneath her
eyelids, trekking rapidly down her face. She heard
the slam of the taxi door, then the roar of the en-
gine as it went down the street. Then silence.

He was gone. Dear God, he was really gone, and
her heart ached with a pain she feared was lethal.
She'd experienced the pain once before, when Bill
had died. But at that time she'd known the separation had been out of their hands, had been con-
trolled by fate. But this...this separation from Nick
was created by his fears, his unshakable disbelief in
the magic of love. It seemed so unfair, so damned
frustrating.

She swiped at her cheeks and took a deep breath,
becoming aware of a strange noise coming from
Rachel's bedroom. She started up the stairs, and
the noise became recognizable as she drew closer.
It was the sound of Rachel weeping.

Rapping softly on Rachel's door, she opened it
and went in, surprised to see the little girl leaning

out the window. She was sobbing uncontrollably and emptying her bag of pixie dust out the window.

"Rachel, sweetie. What are you doing?" Violet walked over to stand next to Rachel by the window, watching as the red glitter took flight in the early-morning breeze. "Honey, why are you throwing your pixie dust away?" she asked softly.

"It doesn't work," Rachel cried, releasing another handful out the window. "It's not really magic. It's just dumb old glitter." She dumped the last of it, then turned to Violet, her cheeks streaked with tears, her blue eyes muddied with misery. "I told you it was pixie dust, but it wasn't. It was really daddy dust. The pixies brought it for me, and I sprinkled and sprinkled Nick." Her lower lip trembled again. "But he didn't turn into my daddy." With another choked sob, she threw herself into Violet's arms.

Violet held her daughter close, stroking the baby-fine hair, tears misting her own vision as she tried to find the words that would console the little girl's broken heart. But the words wouldn't come. How could she heal Rachel's heart when her own was broken in two?

Chapter Ten

Violet watched the real-estate agent banging the For Sale sign into her front yard, a curious mixture of relief and panic sweeping through her.

Mrs. Jefferson finished the task, then turned and smiled brightly at Violet. "I'll be in touch as soon as we get a nibble on the house. I'm sure it will go fast. These old homes are so popular." With a wave of the hammer, the plump woman got into her car and drove off.

Violet watched until the car had disappeared from sight, then turned back and stared at the sign. A bittersweet ache welled up in her chest. The sale of the house was the last connection to Bill and his dreams. And yet, she knew it was the right thing to do, had known it for some time. The house was a burden too big for her to shoulder alone.

"So, you finally made up your mind."

Violet turned to see Janet. She smiled at her friend and neighbor. "Yes, I've made up my mind."

Janet walked over and placed an arm around Violet's shoulders. "Joe and the boys are at a ball game. Come on over and let me fix you a tall glass of ice tea. We can talk about this momentous decision of yours."

Together the two women entered Janet's big, cheery kitchen. Violet sat down at the table and waited for Janet to pour their tea and join her. "It's taken me the last two weeks to come to a final decision," she began once Janet was seated across from her. "But the minute Mrs. Jefferson put the sign in the yard, I knew my decision was a good one. It's time . . . time to move on and get on with my life. I can't do it with that house on my shoulders."

Janet reached across the table and grabbed Violet's hand. "I know selling that house is the best thing for you and Rachel, but I'm going to miss you like crazy."

Violet laughed. "I'm not moving to the moon, just two blocks away."

"I know, but it just won't be the same," Janet replied, releasing Violet's hand. "So, you've definitely decided on the place over on Maple Street?"

Violet nodded. "I'm meeting the real-estate agent there this afternoon for a last look before I make an official offer." She took a sip of her tea, then continued. "The house is a lot smaller than this one, but it's nice and cozy, perfect for Rachel and me. And the good part is it doesn't need any work. It's in move-in condition."

Janet nodded. "Good. You were working yourself to death on that house." She looked at Violet curiously. "Are you sorry you didn't enter the contest last week?"

Violet knew she was talking about the Homes League contest and she slowly shook her head. "No, I'm not sorry." At some point during the course of the past two weeks, the contest had lost its importance, her obsession had died. "I suddenly realized that I was clinging to Bill's dream, afraid of letting it go, scared to face the emptiness I might feel if it was gone." She smiled crookedly at Janet. "I was so mad at Nick for all the things he said to me the night before he left." Violet had related most of the conversation to Janet when Nick had first gone back to Chicago. "But," she continued, "although much of what he said, he knew nothing about...he was right about the house. It has been eating me alive." She sighed, wondering when the mere mention of Nick's name wouldn't hurt anymore.

"How's Rachel?" Janet asked with a frown.

"Still rather subdued and she still refuses to have anything to do with her pixie dust. But she's a survivor. She'll be fine." Violet said this with more conviction than she felt. Both Rachel and her own lives were going through transition. Rachel seemed pleased about their move into the smaller house with the swing set in the backyard, and was excited about picking out a new bedspread and curtains for her new room, but Nick's absence was still a fresh wound, one that only time could possibly heal.

"I could just kick that man," Janet exclaimed, slapping her hands down on the tabletop. "I know he cared about you and Rachel. I've never seen him as happy as he was when he was with the two of you. He's always been so damned stubborn."

Violet shrugged, biting the inside of her mouth to still the tears that, for the past two weeks, had made unexpected, spontaneous appearances. "It doesn't matter now," she said softly. "He just didn't believe in magic. He refused to believe in love."

Nick watched as his client took the stand for cross-examination. As he stared at her, the broad-shouldered, heavily made-up brunette seemed to melt away and a blonde with lavender eyes took her place. For a long moment he gazed hungrily at his mental vision, then with a rapid shake of his head, the vision exploded, becoming once again the hardened features of Christine Bellows, who was suing her husband of eight years for divorce.

He rubbed his eyes tiredly, certain that it was lack of sleep that resulted in his hallucinations. Since returning to Chicago, he'd been working fifteen- and eighteen-hour days. It left him less time to remember a woman who loved him and a little girl who'd called him Daddy.

"I . . . I can't breathe." Mrs. Bellows's asthmatic gasps captured Nick's attention. He'd known of the woman's history of asthma, but this was the first time he'd seen evidence of the problem.

"Your Honor." Nick stood up. "Perhaps we could take a recess?"

The judge called for a fifteen-minute recess, but before Nick could get his client off the stand, she collapsed, gasping and choking for air. Bedlam broke loose. Somebody called the paramedics and within minutes Mrs. Bellows was on a stretcher, stabilized but headed for the hospital where her own doctor was on call.

"She'll be fine," the medic assured Nick as they loaded her into the ambulance. Nick nodded in relief. The medic, a young man shook his head and smiled ruefully. "There are days when I think the whole world is full of sick people and accident victims," he said as he got into the ambulance and they pulled away.

Going back into the courtroom, Nick had the case postponed until Mrs. Bellows was physically able to continue, then he packed up his briefcase and went home to his apartment. The apartment was silent, unwelcoming as he entered. He briefly remembered how welcoming it had always felt to walk into Violet's house, then consciously shoved the thoughts out of his head.

What he needed was a short run around the park. The physical activity always helped to clear his head. He immediately changed into a pair of sweatpants and a T-shirt, then grabbed his running shoes from the floor of the closet.

He sat down on the edge of the bed and slid one shoe on, muttering a curse as he saw that the shoelace was knotted. He worked on the knot, his frown relaxing somewhat as he suddenly remembered something Rachel had told him. Were the pixies angry with him? Was that why nothing seemed to be going right in the past two weeks? Was that why he'd ripped his favorite shirt yesterday? Was that the reason for the knots in his shoelaces?

He smiled and flopped back on the bed, remembering Rachel's impish grin as she dusted him with her magic glitter, the sound of her infectious giggles when he teased her. His smile slowly faded as a vision of Violet filled his mind. He closed his eyes, overwhelmed as memories of her filled his senses. The scent of her perfume... the satiny softness of her skin, the sweetness and heat of her mouth against his... The memories caused an immediate, intense reaction, a sharp, vivid pain in the pit of his stomach. It wasn't just the memories of her physical attractiveness that stirred him. It was also the sound of her laughter, the love and special attention she gave to her daughter, her belief in goodness and magic. She was special...Rachel was special. And for a little while they had made him feel special, too.

The whole world is full of sick people and accident victims. The words of the paramedic whirled around in his head, haunting him, plaguing him with some elusive implication he couldn't quite put his finger on. What was it that bothered him? Why did the paramedic's words play and replay over and over again, as if trying to tell him something important?

He sat up suddenly, the implications crystalizing in his head. He realized now what he needed to do.

Thirty minutes later he was on a plane to Cleveland.

"The furnace was replaced a year ago and there are storm windows all around," Mrs. Jefferson explained for the third time.

Violet nodded absently, walking around the living room, trying to imagine her furniture in place. She would have to sell some things; there was no way this smaller place could accommodate the same furnishings as where she lived now. But the thought didn't bother her.

The house was in perfect shape, ready to be moved into immediately. There were a few things Violet knew she would want to do, like replace the kitchen wallpaper with something more bright and cheery, and she'd promised Rachel they would do her room in whatever colors she chose. Violet felt a tingle of excitement. This time it would be different. She'd do the work she wanted, when she wanted. There would be no driving need to accomplish a near-impossible load.

The house seemed to embrace her, draw her into its coziness and she knew she and Rachel could eventually be happy here. It felt right. It felt good. If only... She shoved the torturous thought aside.

"I think it's perfect."

Violet whirled around at the sound of the familiar deep voice. As she saw him standing in the doorway of the house, she wondered briefly if she'd truly lost her mind, if her wistful thinking had somehow managed to conjure up the likeness of him.

But when he smiled, a tentative one that made him look younger, vulnerable, she realized he wasn't a figment of her imagination, he was real and he was here.

"What . . . what are you doing here?" she asked, surprised that her voice was just a breathless whisper.

"I had to come. The pixies made me." He moved closer to her, enveloping her in his familiar, beloved scent.

"I. . . I think there's something I need to check in the kitchen," Mrs. Jefferson said with a nervous giggle as she disappeared, leaving Violet and Nick alone in the room.

"Violet, the pixies have played havoc in my life for the past two weeks. It's been horrible." He now stood so close to her she could feel the heat emanating from his body, feel the warm sweetness of his breath on her face. "I can't sleep, I can't eat. I spill coffee, lose my car keys—and look at my shoes." He pointed down to his tennis shoes, the shoe strings hopelessly knotted.

"How...how did you know I was here?" She stared at him, afraid to hope, afraid to speculate on his reasons for standing in front of her. She was so frightened of being wrong, so afraid of the hurt if she was mistaken.

"I went by your house and saw the For Sale sign. Janet told me where to find you."

"But I don't understand. Why are you here?"

For the first time since he'd arrived, he touched her. He reached out and took her hand in his and Violet's heart began a rapid tattoo. She was terrified to hope, afraid that another round of shattered dreams would destroy her. "This morning in court, my client collapsed and had to be taken from the room by a paramedic," he began.

"I'm sorry," Violet replied, more confused than anything. He'd flown all this way to discuss with her the health problems of a client? It was true, she had lost her mind, she thought dismally.

"That's not the important part," he continued, squeezing her hands to silence her. "Anyway, as the. paramedic left, he muttered something about the whole world being full of sick people and accident victims. And suddenly I realized that the medic and I had a lot in common. We both had allowed our jobs to become our perceptions of the world. He thinks the world is comprised only of sick people, and I believed the world was made up of only unhappy married people. For the past five years, divorcing couples have been the only personal contact I've had. I worked with them, I ate with them, they interrupted my sleep with their phone calls. They were my life, they were my world…until I came out here." He placed her hand against his heart. "You made me see the possibilities, you made me wonder if maybe there was something more."

"Why have you come back here?" Violet couldn't stand it anymore. She needed to know before her heart beat itself to death in her chest.

"I've come back for the magic, Violet. I've come back for you." His eyes burned with an indigo flame as his hands moved up to her shoulders. "Violet, I love you. I want a life here in Glenville with you and Rachel."

"Oh, Nick." She threw herself into his arms, a sob of happiness catching in her throat.

He placed his hands on either side of her face, tilting it up so he was looking deeply into her eyes. "Will you marry me, Violet? Will you be my wife for the rest of our lives?"

"Yes, oh, yes," she gasped and as his lips claimed hers in a kiss that spoke of tender passion, undying love and magic, her heart filled up with her happiness.

"Does this mean you'll take the house?" Mrs. Jefferson asked, peeking through the doorway of the kitchen.

"Yes," they both said together, then laughed and kissed again.

It took only minutes for them to sign the appropriate papers making an offer on the house, then together they got into Violet's car and headed to Doris's house to pick up Rachel.

"What made you decide to sell your house?" he asked, his hand reaching over to capture hers.

"Your words about me killing myself for a dream that wasn't even one of my own."

Nick winced. "I was out of line."

"Perhaps." She grinned. "But it was true. Like Rachel and her pixie dust, I was holding on to the house and the dream for security. But it was a false security, one that was eating me alive both financially and physically. You were right, at least about that part."

"Violet...I have some money put away...if you wanted to, you know, keep the house, we could," he offered tentatively.

She smiled at him, loving him all the more for his offer. She shook her head. "No. That house belonged to another life, another woman. We'll have our own house and build our own dreams."

Dreams...yes, Nick thought. That was what had always been missing from his life. But as he parked the car and turned to look at Violet, he saw all the dreams of their future, all the love of a lifetime, and he knew he was where he belonged.

As they got out of the car, Rachel exploded out the front door. "Nick!" she cried, her little legs pumping double time until she was close enough to fling herself in his arms. "You came back," she said, throwing her arms around his neck and burying her face into his neck. "You came back!"

Nick felt the warmth of her little body against his, smelled the sweetness of her sun-kissed hair and he was so filled with his love, he couldn't speak for a moment.

He smiled at Doris, who'd come out of the door to join them. "Sure I came back," he answered Rachel, setting her back down on the ground. "Even a pixie princess needs a daddy."

Rachel's eyes widened at his words. "You're going to be my daddy?"

"I sure am," Nick answered. "That is, if you want me to be."

"You promise?" she pressed.

"Cross my heart and hope to die," Nick replied, his gaze meeting Violet's in an unspoken vow of commitment.

"Oh, boy," Rachel squealed with glee. "I've got a daddy!" She turned to Doris and grabbed her hand. "Come on, Mimi. We've got to cook another pixie pie."

"My heavens, whatever for?" Doris laughed.

Rachel tugged her down and whispered in her ear, then ran for the front door. "Come on, Mimi." She disappeared inside.

Doris turned to Violet and Nick, her blue eyes sparkling with merriment. "I guess I'd better get in there. Rachel has a new order for the pixies."

"What on earth can she want now?" Violet asked. "She's going to have a new house and a new daddy."

Doris nodded and grinned at them. "I suppose I'd better tell you what she wants because I'm going to need your cooperation on this one." Her grin widened. "The daddy dust worked so well that now Rachel has decided to ask the pixies for some baby brother dust." With a cackle of delight, Doris headed inside the house.

"Daddy dust?" Nick looked at Violet.

"The red glitter," Violet explained.

He smiled down at her as he drew her into the circle of his arms. "You know we can't disappoint her."

"About what?"

"About this baby brother stuff." He leaned down and kissed the end of her nose. "I think it's something we need to get to work on as soon as possible." He kissed the side of her neck, just below her ear, causing shivers of pleasure to dance up her spine. "I love you, Violet Sanders," he breathed as his lips claimed hers in a kiss that promised a lifetime of loving and magic to spare.

*   *   *   *   *

HE'S MORE THAN A MAN, HE'S ONE OF OUR

Fabulous Fathers

MAD ABOUT MAGGIE
by Pepper Adams

All at once, Dan Lucas was a father—and a grandfather! But opening his arms to his grandson didn't guarantee that he'd find a place in his son's life. And the child's aunt, Maggie Mayhew, would do anything in her power to keep Dan out of her family. But could she keep Dan out of her heart?

Available in October from Silhouette Romance.

Fall in love with our **Fabulous Fathers!**

FF1093

Silhouette
ROMANCE™

OFFICIAL RULES • MILLION DOLLAR SWEEPSTAKES
NO PURCHASE OR OBLIGATION NECESSARY TO ENTER

To enter, follow the directions published. **ALTERNATE MEANS OF ENTRY:** Hand print your name and address on a 3"x5" card and mail to either: Silhouette "Match 3," 3010 Walden Ave., P.O. Box 1867, Buffalo, NY 14269-1867, or Silhouette "Match 3," P.O. Box 609, Fort Erie, Ontario L2A 5X3, and we will assign your Sweepstakes numbers. (Limit: one entry per envelope.) For eligibility, entries must be received no later than March 31, 1994. No responsibility is assumed for lost, late or misdirected entries.

Upon receipt of entry, Sweepstakes numbers will be assigned. To determine winners, Sweepstakes numbers will be compared against a list of randomly preselected prizewinning numbers. In the event all prizes are not claimed via the return of prizewinning numbers, random drawings will be held from among all other entries received to award unclaimed prizes.

Prizewinners will be determined no later than May 30, 1994. Selection of winning numbers and random drawings are under the supervision of D.L. Blair, Inc., an independent judging organization, whose decisions are final. One prize to a family or organization. No substitution will be made for any prize, except as offered. Taxes and duties on all prizes are the sole responsibility of winners. Winners will be notified by mail. Chances of winning are determined by the number of entries distributed and received.

Sweepstakes open to persons 18 years of age or older, except employees and immediate family members of Torstar Corporation, D.L. Blair, Inc., their affiliates, subsidiaries and all other agencies, entities and persons connected with the use, marketing or conduct of this Sweepstakes. All applicable laws and regulations apply. Sweepstakes offer void wherever prohibited by law. Any litigation within the province of Quebec respecting the conduct and awarding of a prize in this Sweepstakes must be submitted to the Régies des Loteries et Courses du Quebec. In order to win a prize, residents of Canada will be required to correctly answer a time-limited arithmetical skill-testing question. Values of all prizes are in U.S. currency.

Winners of major prizes will be obligated to sign and return an affidavit of eligibility and release of liability within 30 days of notification. In the event of non-compliance within this time period, prize may be awarded to an alternate winner. Any prize or prize notification returned as undeliverable will result in the awarding of that prize to an alternate winner. By acceptance of their prize, winners consent to use of their names, photographs or other likenesses for purposes of advertising, trade and promotion on behalf of Torstar Corporation without further compensation, unless prohibited by law.

This Sweepstakes is presented by Torstar Corporation, its subsidiaries and affiliates in conjunction with book, merchandise and/or product offerings. Prizes are as follows: Grand Prize—$1,000,000 (payable at $33,333.33 a year for 30 years). First through Sixth Prizes may be presented in different creative executions, each with the following approximate values: First Prize—$35,000; Second Prize—$10,000; 2 Third Prizes—$5,000 each; 5 Fourth Prizes—$1,000 each; 10 Fifth Prizes—$250 each; 1,000 Sixth Prizes—$100 each. Prizewinners will have the opportunity of selecting any prize offered for that level. A travel-prize option, if offered and selected by winner, must be completed within 12 months of selection and is subject to hotel and flight accommodations availability. Torstar Corporation may present this Sweepstakes utilizing names other than Million Dollar Sweepstakes. For a current list of all prize options offered within prize levels and all names the Sweepstakes may utilize, send a self-addressed, stamped envelope (WA residents need not affix return postage) to: Million Dollar Sweepstakes Prize Options/Names, P.O. Box 4710, Blair, NE 68009.

The Extra Bonus Prize will be awarded in a random drawing to be conducted no later than May 30, 1994 from among all entries received. To qualify, entries must be received by March 31, 1994 and comply with published directions. No purchase necessary. For complete rules, send a self-addressed, stamped envelope (WA residents need not affix return postage) to: Extra Bonus Prize Rules, P.O. Box 4600, Blair, NE 68009.

For a list of prizewinners (available after July 31, 1994) send a separate, stamped, self-addressed envelope to: Million Dollar Sweepstakes Winners, P.O. Box 4728, Blair, NE 68009.

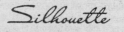

Silhouette
R O M A N C E™

The miracle of love is waiting to be discovered in Duncan, Oklahoma! Arlene James takes you there in her trilogy, THIS SIDE OF HEAVEN. Look for Book Two in October!

AN OLD-FASHIONED LOVE

Traci Temple was settling in just fine to small-town life—until she got involved with Wyatt Gilley and his two rascal sons. Though Wyatt's love was tempting, it was dangerous. Traci wasn't willing to play house without wedding vows. But how could she hope to spend her life with a man who swore never to marry again?

Available in October, only from Silhouette Romance!

Silhouette Books has done it again!

Opening night in October has never been as exciting! Come watch as the curtain rises and romance flourishes when the stars of tomorrow make their debuts today!

Revel in Jodi O'Donnell's STILL SWEET ON HIM—
Silhouette Romance #969
...as Callie Farrell's renovation of the family homestead leads her straight into the arms of teenage crush Drew Barnett!

Tingle with Carol Devine's BEAUTY AND THE BEASTMASTER—
Silhouette Desire #816
...as legal eagle Amanda Tarkington is carried off by wrestler Bram Masterson!

Thrill to Elyn Day's A BED OF ROSES—
Silhouette Special Edition #846
...as Dana Whitaker's body and soul are healed by sexy physical therapist Michael Gordon!

Believe when Kylie Brant's McLAIN'S LAW —
Silhouette Intimate Moments #528
...takes you into detective Connor McLain's life as he falls for psychic—and suspect—Michele Easton!

Catch the classics of tomorrow—*premiering* today—
only from ▼ *Silhouette*

If you're looking for more titles by

CARLA CASSIDY,

don't miss these heartwarming stories by one of
Silhouette's most popular authors:

Silhouette Desire®

#05784	A FLEETING MOMENT	$2.89	☐

Silhouette Romance™

#08884	FIRE AND SPICE	$2.69	☐
#08905	HOMESPUN HEARTS	$2.69	☐
#08924	GOLDEN GIRL	$2.69	☐
#08942	SOMETHING NEW	$2.75	☐

Silhouette Shadows™

#27004	SWAMP SECRETS	$3.50	☐
#27011	HEART OF THE BEAST	$3.50	☐

TOTAL AMOUNT $
POSTAGE & HANDLING $
($1.00 for one book, 50¢ for each additional)
APPLICABLE TAXES* $ _____
TOTAL PAYABLE $ _____
(check or money order—please do not send cash)

To order, complete this form and send it, along with a check or money order for the total above,
payable to Silhouette Books, to: *In the U.S.:* 3010 Walden Avenue, P.O. Box 9077, Buffalo,
NY 14269-9077; *In Canada:* P.O. Box 636, Fort Erie, Ontario, L2A 5X3.

Name: _____

Address: _____ City: _____

State/Prov.: _____ Zip/Postal Code: _____

*New York residents remit applicable sales taxes.
Canadian residents remit applicable GST and provincial taxes.   CCBACK1